Nina realized her heart was in her throat. The fire was consuming one side of the house, but it wouldn't be long before it was destroying all of it. Movement flashed in front of the window next to the front door.

A loud crack split through the air. The left side of the house shuddered. Flames spiked higher in the air as half of the roof crumbled.

"Caleb!"

Nina ran around the house. The back door was wide open. Smoke had already filled the inside.

"Caleb," she tried again, taking an uncertain step forward. She couldn't hear anything else over the fire burrowing into the structure. No one moved.

Terror clawed at Nina's heart. Then she thought about her mom.

Bolstered by thoughts of her mother and two of the bluest eyes she'd seen, Nina covered her mouth and nose with her arm and ran into the cabin.

REINING IN TROUBLE

TYLER ANNE SNELL

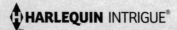

HARLEQUIN INTRIGUE®

This book is for Girl Group. Virginia, you continue to be fierce. Faith, you continue to be crafty. Jasmine, you continue to be true. Thanks for always being ready to lift others up when life tries to push them down. You're all absolute queens!

ISBN-13: 978-1-335-60443-9

Reining in Trouble

Recycling programs
for this product may
not exist in your area.

Copyright © 2019 by Tyler Anne Snell

Printed in U.S.A.

Tyler Anne Snell genuinely loves all genres of the written word. However, she's realized that she loves books filled with sexual tension and mysteries a little more than the rest. Her stories have a good dose of both. Tyler lives in Alabama with her same-named husband and their mini "lions." When she isn't reading or writing, she's playing video games and working on her blog, *Almost There*. To follow her shenanigans, visit tylerannesnell.com.

Books by Tyler Anne Snell

Harlequin Intrigue

Winding Road Redemption

Reining in Trouble

The Protectors of Riker County

Small-Town Face-Off
The Deputy's Witness
Forgotten Pieces
Loving Baby
The Deputy's Baby
The Negotiation

Orion Security

Private Bodyguard
Full Force Fatherhood
Be on the Lookout: Bodyguard
Suspicious Activities

Manhunt

Visit the Author Profile page at Harlequin.com.

CAST OF CHARACTERS

Caleb Nash—As one of the Nash triplets who were abducted all those years ago with no reason why, this detective has turned his focus to helping others get the answers he's never had. However, when the entrancing new addition to his family's ranch finds herself the center of someone's dangerous fascination, can this cowboy solve a mystery that's been slowly burning through their town?

Nina Drake—After a tragedy that flipped her life upside down, this transplant from Florida is just trying to live her life beneath the radar. Taking a job at the Nash Family Ranch's new retreat, she's ready to focus on work and nothing else. But from one misunderstanding with the handsome detective to the unmistakable attack against her, there's no denying that someone isn't ready to let her live her new life.

Madeline & Desmond Nash—As two of the triplets, Madi and Desmond are fiercely loyal to each other, Caleb and their family.

Declan Nash—Sheriff and the triplets' older brother, this lawman must stay on his toes to keep their home and town from going up in flames.

Jasmine "Jazz" Santiago—Fellow detective and Caleb's best friend, this detective always has her partner's back.

Dorothy Nash—The Nash family matriarch has seen her fair share of heartbreak but always reminds her children to stay optimistic.

Delores Dearborn—A local reporter becomes tangled in the mystery overtaking the town. Is she a victim or the mastermind?

Chapter One

Detective Caleb Nash switched his jeans for jogging shorts and hoped to high heaven no one he knew saw him. It was a particularly pleasant day in Overlook. The humidity was down and the heat wasn't too bad. He'd have to clean the pollen off of his truck before he went to the department unless he wanted his partner, Jazz, to give him grief again. She always reminded him that they represented the sheriff's department, vehicles included. It was easy for her to say. She drove an obnoxious gray four-door that barely showed any pollen. Not to mention her husband detailed cars for a living.

Caleb drove an old dark blue pickup that showed every speck of yellow, and as for a spouse with a helpful job? His last girlfriend had split because the only real marriage he was interested in was to his job. Her words, not his. Though he couldn't deny they held some truth. She'd also never been a fan of small-town Tennessee. The last thing she'd be worried about was him driving around town with a pollen-coated junker.

Though that insignificant mark of shame would be nothing compared to what would be said if any of Overlook's residents saw one of the Nash triplets jogging in the *short* shorts he was currently sporting. Good, bad, or embarrassing, the town already had enough to talk about when it came to the family. Adding his bare legs to the mix was something he wanted to avoid. Never mind keeping the sheriff away from the image. *That* grief would last for months longer.

But what was a man supposed to do?

The reappearance of his short shorts from track in school had been his mama's fault. Her latest drop-in had resulted in a surge of spring cleaning he hadn't asked for but couldn't stop. The casualty in the latest cleaning war had been the accidental destruction of his normal workout wear. Now he was popping in his earbuds at the mouth of Connor's Trail with more skin than he was comfortable showing, hoping that none of the people living or working on the Nash Family Ranch would find themselves up that way.

On a scale of one to five, one being a kid-friendly walk meant to enjoy the scenery and five being a laborious attempt at training for trails that went up the Rockies, Connor's Trail was a three. It began where the woods that were scattered across the back half of the hundred acres of ranchland curved, forming a crescent-moon shape that rose and dipped the farther you went inside the tree line. The uneven terrain warranted several new signs warning guests from the Wild Iris Retreat to be careful. Caleb knew for a fact that there were three in total surrounding the trail because he'd been the one to stake them in the ground. It was supposed to have been his brother, Declan, who did the deed, but work had pulled him away. There wasn't much Caleb could do about that. He could argue until he was blue in the face with his eldest brother, but he didn't dare try the same tactic with the sheriff. Even if they were one and the same.

Caleb leaned into the beat of his music as thoughts of his brother led to thoughts about work. Caleb had been a detective with the Wildman County Sheriff's Department for five years. In that time he'd learned the importance of routine, especially when it came to exercising.

"There's never enough time to do every *single* thing you want to," his father, Michael, used to say. "But there's always time to do at least one thing. You just have to make that one thing count."

While his siblings, Madeline and Desmond, thought that was a bunch of bologna, Caleb had taken his late father's words to heart. That mantra had served the patriarch well throughout his life.

Until it hadn't.

But that hadn't been his fault.

Caleb's thoughts started to darken. The upbeat music did little to stave off that darkness. No matter how many years passed, Caleb knew there would always be moments where what had happened clawed its way to the forefront of his mind. Where it would sit. And wait.

A horrifying collection of memories from what felt like a different lifetime. The Nash triplets stuck in a loop of helplessness, fear, and pain.

His feet dug into the dirt as he made physical distance from the home behind him. It had taken years for him, Madi, or Desmond to go back into the woods. To move between the trees without fear. Without worry.

Yet, sometimes, when Caleb thought about his father he couldn't help but think about the man with the scar along his hand. Then, suddenly, Caleb was a child again. He'd hear Madi scream. Hear Desmond cry out in pain. He'd hear his own voice quaver in anger and fear.

Then Caleb would remember that, even though the memories felt so real sometimes, that's all they were. Memories. Ones that had no place on the ranch at the end of Winding Road.

"But, how can it be over if the man with the scar is still out there?" asked Caleb's inner voice. It was a question that always followed the memories, darkening them even further.

Today, though, Caleb refused to entertain them for long. He leaned into the beat of his music and focused on the comfort of routine.

The burn of exertion didn't kick in until Caleb was passing the third mile marker. Scots pines lined either side of the dirty trail, their roots gnarled and reaching every few yards. Caleb had run the trail since he was fifteen and knew when to jump over or step around the ones that threatened to take a jogger by surprise. Just as he knew the exact spot to veer off the beaten path and forge over a less-known one to his favorite place across all of the ranch. The trees clustered closer but Caleb wove around them and kept going.

He heard the stream before he saw the water.

The trees thinned out and the ground dipped. Caleb jumped off a dirt ledge and slapped the trunk of a tree that had his initials carved into it. Rocks worn by erosion lined flowing water that was clear enough to see more rocks making up the bottom in the distance. It wasn't a particularly wide waterway, neither was it that deep, but it was always cold.

Caleb was already thinking about stripping down, wading to the deepest point and dunking under for a quick refresher before he rounded the last line of trees. He stopped in his tracks. He wasn't the only one who had been thinking the same thing.

A woman was already standing in the middle of the stream. Her back was turned to him but there was no denying the top layer of her clothes was somewhere else. Her raven-black hair was twisted up and showed smooth tanned skin, bare and reflected in the water just over her waist. Caleb couldn't tell if she had any bottoms on but thought it ungentlemanly to find out. Though he wasn't above admitting that, even from his limited view, there was an attractive curve to the woman. It brought out a feeling of curiosity that mingled with a more intimate excitement, but he wasn't about to search out that feeling. Not when the woman had no idea she was being watched.

Caleb started to backtrack but whatever cool he'd had on the trail had been lost due to the new scenery. He missed his step and grunted as he tried to catch himself from falling. A splash of water was followed quickly by a gasp. Caleb's palm bit into the smaller rocks on the shore. He managed to get his balance from them and went back to standing tall.

Now *he* was the one with an audience.

The woman had sunk down so far that the water was only an inch below her face. If that very same face hadn't been scowling at him, as red as a cherry, Caleb might have taken an extra beat to appreciate the beauty of her sharp features, dimpled cheeks and dark brown eyes. As it was, he barely had the time to defend himself.

And even that he did poorly.

"Before you get any ideas," he called, raising his hands in surrender. "I was on a run. I didn't know anyone would be here."

The woman, who he placed around late twenties, stayed red hot. Even her words had heat to them.

"Heck of a place for a run," she yelled, motioning with one hand around them. The other he assumed was fastened across her chest.

Her implication that he was lying transferred some of that heat to Caleb. He crossed his own arms over his chest.

"I was running on the trail but decided to come and cool off," he defended himself. "This is the deepest part of the stream."

"How *convenient*," she replied with bite. Her eyes skirted to a log that had been on its side for the better part of two years a few feet away from him. Caleb saw a pile of clothes and a pair of tennis shoes on top of it. "Could you please look away now? Or does that take away part of your fun?"

Caleb rolled his eyes, once again not liking the insinuation that he had been lying about his intentions, and made a show of turning all the way around.

"Just so you know, I've been coming to this stream for almost two decades. In all of that time I've never run into another soul."

The woman's feet slapped against the rocks behind him as she ran for her clothes. When she spoke he could tell she was struggling into them as fast as she could go.

"I was out checking the trail, if you must know. I was also specifically told that no one is supposed to be out here for another week," she tried. "Especially not walking the woods."

That got the detective side of Caleb prickling. The only people who'd been given rules on the ranch were employees and he sure didn't remember meeting her. And, he was fairly certain he would have remembered.

"And who told you that?"

"The owners. I work here," she said with pride. "So I suggest you get on your way before I report you to them."

Caleb snorted.

"I wouldn't be so smug about it," she added. "One of them happens to be the sheriff. I don't think he'd look too kindly on Peeping Toms and liars."

"You're right, Declan doesn't like liars," he said, feeling that heat again. He'd never been accused of such a crude thing. The only women he'd been interested in seeing naked he'd let them know, not stalked them off to the side. "He doesn't care for trespassers, either. The ranch might be open but it's private property."

He chanced turning around. The woman was fully dressed in an outfit that gave credence to her claim of exercising. Her eyes drifted down to his shorts before they were back staring defiantly at him.

The resolve she'd been swinging cracked with uncertainty. Still, she held her shoulders back and her chin high. She actually huffed.

"*I'm* not trespassing. I'm coordinator for the Wild Iris Retreat. I just started last week."

A snatch of conversation flitted through Caleb's memory. His mom had been asking Madeline if she would be willing to show the new girl around town a few weeks back. That had been at the height of the Keaton case. He'd barely been around the Retreat since he'd finished the job. While they all had a stake in the Retreat, his mother was the one who ran the technical details, including the hiring. Though he still was hard-pressed to believe the woman scowling at him. All of the Nash family had agreed they wanted to hire locally. It was hard to pass on a genuine experience if the Retreat was being run by an outsider.

He ran a hand across the back of his neck. It was covered in sweat. The water sure would have felt good but he doubted the woman would stand for him stripping, too, and walking into it. He settled for leveling with her.

"I don't remember the job being open for anyone who wasn't local," he said honestly.

A flicker of emotion he couldn't decipher crossed her expression. Her scowl deepened.

"Dorothy said I gave one hell of an interview," she shot back.

For a moment they just looked at each other. This time it was Caleb's certainty that wavered. He believed the woman was telling the truth.

"Well I never like to doubt my mother's decisions."

The woman's face pinballed between surprise, disbelief, embarrassment and stubbornness. Somehow she fell between all of them when she spoke.

"You're one of the triplets."

"In the flesh."

NINA DRAKE FELT like a damned idiot.

She'd spent the last two weeks practicing what she'd say when she met the family whose ranch she was now employed by, desperate to make a great first impression. Not that she thought she'd make a bad one without the practice but because she desperately wanted the job. She *needed* it. So she'd gone over enough scenarios in her head about how she'd meet Dorothy Nash and her four children that by the time Nina had met the mother she'd been cool and confident.

Dorothy had smiled with her, laughed at Nina's attempt at humor and even praised her work ethic.

Preparation had been *key*.

Meeting one of her sons while taking a topless dip and then immediately accusing him of being a creep?

That certainly wasn't the key to anything other than a world of embarrassment.

"I'm Caleb Nash," he continued while she continued to scramble for the right thing to say to make the last five minutes disappear. He was still grinning, which only made everything worse. "I'd prefer Caleb and not Tom, if you please."

The burn of embarrassment that had crawled up her neck was now a steady flame across her cheeks. Still, Nina couldn't just stand there any longer without saying a word. On reflex she cleared her throat and pasted on a smile that felt tight.

"I'm sorry," she said, hoping she sounded at least marginally regretful. She still wasn't convinced the man hadn't been trying to enjoy the free view. Nina might have liked Dorothy but she had yet to meet her sons. One, she knew, was the sheriff. The other two were a part of the triplets. Past that she hadn't heard anything about their jobs or personal lives. Dorothy had kept close to the topic of work. "I guess it wasn't the best idea to go exploring. I thought for sure I would be alone." She strode forward and stretched out her hand. "I'm Nina. Nina Drake."

Caleb's grip was strong and warm. Not that she expected the man in front of her to offer anything less. His arms and legs were toned and muscled, both threatening to break out of the tight shirt he wore and the shorts he barely had on. Even without the show of muscles he just seemed like a man who was sturdy. Well over six feet and broad shouldered, he made Nina feel more than petite next to him.

It didn't help that she was already feeling small because of embarrassment. It *also* didn't help that Caleb had a good-looking grin that matched an extremely handsome face. When Nina had applied for a job on the ranch she'd pictured rugged men in cowboy hats roaming around the property on horses. Not the clean-shaven, dark-haired man wearing short shorts in the middle of the woods in front of her.

Not those baby blues focused solely on her.

Half of the reason she'd taken the job was to curb excitement like this.

Not that *this* was anything more than an awkward situation.

Still, she couldn't imagine being in the presence of the triplets if they had been identical. It would, she suspected, be intimidating to say the least.

"Well, nice to meet you, Nina," he said after their hands had fallen. "I'm sorry I interrupted. I usually stop here to cool off."

Nina was already backing away in the direction she'd originally come. She shook her head and waved off the concern.

"It was my fault," she tried. "I was just trying to familiarize myself with the trails before guests started arriving. I should have stayed on the path." Caleb looked like he was going to say something but she was already retreating into the tree line. "Enjoy your dip," she called. Then she turned on her heel and hurried back to the dirt trail.

It wasn't until she had passed the one-mile marker that she slowed enough to catch her breath. Instead of seeing the humor in the situation, Nina couldn't shake the feeling that she'd almost cost herself a chance at a fresh start.

She balled her hands into fists, resolve to be the perfect employee flooding through her. Not only would she stick strictly to the rules, she decided, but she would also avoid the man who had caught her breaking them.

A branch snapped somewhere off to her side. Nina's blush surged back up her neck, heating her skin, at the thought of Caleb following her. However, as she paused to look between the trees, she saw no one.

Nina finished the trail with a little more urgency in her step, all the while reasoning that the outline of the man she thought she'd seen was just her imagination.

Simply a ghost from her former life.

Chapter Two

The Wild Iris Retreat was a new build on the Nash Family Ranch but it by no means looked out of place. Four cabins were spaced out for privacy and were placed near a network of trails that led to the best fishing on the land, the horse barn for riding lessons or trail riding and a field where, according to Dorothy, one had the best views of the stars.

The main building that housed the Retreat's operations, as well as Nina's office and apartment, was the only part of Wild Iris that had been original to the earlier generation of Nashes. After a flood had forced Dorothy's grandparents to build a new house a good five-minute drive up the road, the old family home had sat in ruins until the idea of the Retreat had been born. It was now standing tall, repurposed and very much alive. While it wasn't as cozy as the cabins near it, Nina couldn't help but favor it above the others.

It reminded her of her mother, if she was being honest. Warm, worn and beautiful.

Nina jogged around to the back door and pulled the key from the waist of her athletic shorts. She slipped her shoes off and carried them through the back hallway to the stairs that branched off what used to be the old living room. The second floor was modest, converted into a studio apartment. It had been created for the manager of the Retreat. Dorothy had wanted the guests to have full access to them without the need to trek up the road to the main house or even farther to two of the Nash sons' houses.

The Nash sons…

Caleb.

Nina stepped into the shower, trying to physically move away from the embarrassment that had overtaken her again. She remembered a time when she had been great at first impressions. *Charming*, according to her father, *intriguing* as a compliment from her mother. At a young age Nina had decided she wanted to use those traits to follow in her mother's footsteps. Maybe become an inspirational speaker for nonprofits too, traveling the state to talk at schools and other organizations.

But then everything had changed.

Nina's mood darkened until nothing but the echo of sadness pinged in her heart. She finished her shower, dressed in a pair of jeans and a button-up, and walked downstairs to the front of the house. Another key unlocked the two spaces of her living quarters and the business side of the retreat and soon she was trying her best not to stew on how cruel life could be sometimes while settling in behind her desk.

The Wild Iris Retreat could be one of many things for guests. If they wanted to relax while feeling like they were in the wilderness, the retreat had beautiful scenery and peace and quiet for them to enjoy. If guests wanted to feel like they were a part of the authentic ranch life, there were horses to ride, trails to adventure on, and a small town where everyone knew everyone else to visit. It could be anything and Nina was there to create more options for it and future guests.

The retreat would be opening in two weeks. Nina had already been there for seven days. In that time she'd worked alongside the manager of daily operations, Molly, and the cook, Roberto. Molly was married to the horse trainer and both lived just outside of the ranch. Nina only got the option to live in the old house because Molly and her husband had had no interest in the space upstairs when they had their own home already. Roberto lived in Overlook but because of the set meal schedule didn't need to be around 24/7 either. So it had been Nina's perk alone to savor. Not only did she not have to deal with the hassle of finding a place to live, her commute had been reduced to nothing.

She brought up her email and read through a few informational ones from Molly and then reached out to local stores asking about any events they might have coming up. It was her job to stay up-to-date with the small town's entertainment so she could always have options for guests who wanted to explore locally. She'd already spoken to a few business owners but at least half of the town's shops didn't have email addresses listed. Or websites, for that matter. If she was going to talk to them, she'd have to do it in person. By the time her email refreshed and a new message popped up in her inbox, Nina was still thinking about going into town and making small talk. She clicked on it, wondering how to be polite but keep her distance as she met the locals, as an image loaded on the screen.

Nina's breath caught.

It was a picture of her. And not just any picture.

She was standing in a stream, back to the camera, but obviously not wearing a top. It was from that morning. No less than a few hours ago.

Her blood went cold at the text in the body of the email.

And everyone thought you were a nice girl.

CALEB STOOD BACK and looked at his handiwork. His truck was gleaming. The pollen was seeping into the mud. He'd thought about going into town and running through the automated car wash at the gas station but had needed the water hose to cool off. He'd decided against using the stream and instead had run the rest of the trail hot. By the time he'd driven home, on the exact opposite side of the ranch, Caleb had been desperate for quick relief. He'd stripped down to nothing but his short shorts and rinsed himself off before working on the truck.

By the time he was done his skin was already dry.

The pleasant day had turned angry. If he hadn't already been tan from living his free time outside, Caleb might have burned beneath the constant shine and heat. He doused himself once more before cutting the water off. He'd use the time between now and when he was dry to finally fix the porch swing he'd been meaning to repair for the last year or so. He'd never used it much but his mother had insisted. If there was ever any one thing true about Dorothy Nash it was her love for porch swings.

Caleb went around back to the shed and grabbed his tools. He was walking across the side yard when an unfamiliar car came barreling up the road. He cursed beneath his breath at not having changed out of his obnoxious shorts as soon as he'd gotten home and hoped once again it wasn't anyone from the department.

No such luck. It was the only person he would have liked to avoid more than his brothers. Caleb dropped his tools on the wraparound porch and groaned.

"Well, howdy-do there, Mr. Nash!"

Jasmine "Jazz" Santiago came out of the car smiling for all she was worth. As a transplant from Portland, she had done a fine job of fitting into Overlook, the department and even the ranch on the occasions she'd stopped by over the last five years. Tall, thin and with a complexion she once had called *smooth mocha*, she was one half of their mismatched detective pair. While Caleb erred on the side of contemplation and quiet, Jazz was blunt and always ready to be heard. Even now she cut the engine and bounded toward him, laughing.

"I'd always wondered what you *really* did on your off days," she continued, motioning to his bare chest and shorts, and then pointing toward the tool box. "I never would have guessed you were working on an audition for one of the Village People."

Caleb groaned again.

"First of all, that's a throwback," he said, leaning into the teasing. "If I was auditioning for anything it'd clearly be something *Magic Mike*-related." Jazz laughed as Caleb searched out his shirt. He tugged it over his head while Jazz inspected his freshly washed truck. She seemed to approve. "Now, other than coming out here to roast me, what's up?"

Jazz switched moods in a flash. Work mode crinkled her brow together. She met his stare with severity.

"I tried calling but the sheriff told me just to go ahead and come out here. I was already out test-driving Brando's new car so it worked out easier." Brando was Jazz's husband and the fact that she hadn't brought him along felt even more foreboding. Caleb felt himself go on alert. Not only that but Declan was a stickler about privacy. Even more so about privacy when his staff was off the clock. That he'd sent Jazz out wasn't a good sign. She pulled her phone out and swiped until she got to the picture she wanted. "When's the last time you went out to the Overlook Pass behind Nancy Calder's house?"

Nancy Calder had been a staple in the community for longer than Caleb had been alive. Her father opened the local grocery store thirty years ago. Now, her son ran it. She had a farm with some acreage out near the Overlook town limits, but after turning ninety she'd moved out of state to be with her daughter. Part of her land was rented out to cattle farmers but no one lived in the house. Overlook Pass was a bridge just outside of her property line that had been given historic status. No one used it for transportation but tourists liked taking pictures of it and fishing the water beneath it. The last time Caleb had visited either place had been with his ex, well over a year ago. He said as much to Jazz.

She handed her phone over.

"Apparently no one has been out there for a while."

The picture was all wrong. Where there should have been an aged but beautiful bridge there was now bits of charred wood and nothing else.

"What the—" he started, anger threatening to become hotter than the weather. "Did…did someone *burn* it?"

Jazz nodded.

"The fire chief is heading that way now to investigate but, so far, there's no way to know if this happened recently or a while back. Which may or may not be related to this." She took back her phone and swiped to another picture. "Last night there was a house fire out on Brookewood Drive. They're still investigating if it was arson or not. It might not be connected but Declan's telling everyone in the department to keep their eyes open, just in case."

Caleb didn't blame his brother for the department-wide warning. Or the urgency with which he'd deployed the caution. Overlook had a fair amount of forest stretching around it. Arson was always a threat everyone took seriously. One match could make a devastating difference. Plus, Brookewood Drive was a five or so minute drive from the burned bridge. He would have done the same thing in Declan's place.

Once Jazz had said her piece she hopped back into her car and raised a cloud of dust as she left on the dirt road. Caleb returned to his toolbox but he didn't feel the same ambition to attend to the broken swing as he had before.

The burning of an unused bridge was something he'd take over a home or business burning down any day. Yet he couldn't stop the stab of loss in his chest. His father had loved that bridge. He'd taken Caleb and his siblings there at least once a month to fish when it was the season. It had become a routine that Caleb had hoped at a young age they'd keep as he got older. Although that plan had changed due to circumstances no one had seen coming, Caleb still thought fondly about their time there.

Now it was just another part of his father that had been chipped away by a senseless act.

Caleb abandoned the toolbox and showered off. He returned his missed calls—Declan and his mother, the only people who ever seemed to call him nowadays—and decided to live dangerously and crack open a beer with his lunch. He was about to go out to the porch to enjoy it when another car crept up and stopped just behind his truck. This time he was ready for possible company. His short shorts had officially been retired. Now he was in his favorite pair of blue jeans and sporting a beige Stetson cowboy hat he'd bought himself for Christmas.

The driver's side door swung open just as he placed his full beer down on the porch railing. For the smallest of moments Caleb didn't recognize the woman barreling toward him. Then, as her petite frame got closer, he fully remembered seeing that very same scowl only hours beforehand.

Nina Drake most certainly looked like she had a bone to pick.

"Well, how do you—" he started, hoping to keep whatever fuse she had unlit by making a better second impression than he had the first. However, Nina wasn't having it. Her cheeks were flushed red and her chest was rising and falling much faster than was normal. She crossed her arms and interrupted him with fire in her eyes.

"And here I thought *you* were a nice *guy*," she said, voice high. "There I was feeling bad for our little misunderstanding earlier, but now? Now I should report you to the authorities!"

Caleb raised his hands in defense, of what he wasn't sure. His eyebrow slid up in question.

"Excuse me?"

Nina was close enough now that he could see the freckles across her cheeks and the bridge of her nose— barely there in the shadows of the trees but undeniable in the full force of the sun. Her nostrils were flared, her fists were balled. Caleb almost took a step back, worried she was readying for an attack.

"Not only were you *watching* me at the water, you took my picture," she said, voice dipping into nothing but ice. "And I came here to make sure you delete that picture or I will go straight to the sheriff *and* your mother."

Caleb lowered his hands. Any amusement he'd felt was long gone.

"I told you, I wasn't spying on you. I've been going to that spot on my runs since I was fifteen. I was just as surprised to see someone there as you were. And I sure as hell didn't take any pictures."

A small look of relief passed across Nina's expression. It was quickly replaced by one he'd seen in the eyes of countless people during his career in law enforcement.

Fear.

"Nina, what happened?" Caleb pressed. "What pictures are you talking about?"

She hesitated for a moment. Then met his eyes with concern crowding every bit of dark brown she had in them.

"Someone took a picture of me at the stream today. And they sent it to the Retreat's email."

Caleb's reaction was immediate. He felt every muscle in him go taut.

"What?" he asked through his teeth.

"I can show you on the computer back at the office if you want. That email isn't attached to my phone and I… I didn't want to forward it. I didn't want to look at it anymore."

Her eyes broke contact. She looked down at her hands. It was such a vulnerable action that Caleb had a hard time not venting his disbelief that someone would do such a thing and anger at the person who had right then and there. But then the lawman side of his brain started to kick in.

"Let me get my keys," he said instead. Nina nodded. She was still standing there when he came back out. This time she was staring off toward the fields behind the house. The very same piece of scenery he had been getting ready to enjoy. Tall grass waved lazily in the breeze as if waving hello. Unaware that something was wrong.

"I'll follow you back to your office," he said, breaking the spell she'd fallen under. Her expression was impassive now, yet her question was nothing but troubling.

"Caleb, if you didn't take that picture, who did?"

Chapter Three

Caleb completely forgot about Overlook Pass burning as soon as he saw the email that had been sent to Nina. Not only did the caption make his blood boil, the location from which the picture had been taken had him itching for answers.

"That was right next to where I was when I first saw you." He pointed to the left corner of the picture. Caleb pictured the woods he had grown up knowing like the back of his hand. "Whoever took this was crouched down."

Nina leaned over the back of the office chair to take another look. A few strands of hair escaped her braid. The unmistakable smell of lavender invaded his senses. It caught him off guard.

"It was obviously taken before you showed up," she said, voice calculating and focused. "And not long after I'd first gone in. I had just wanted to cool down. I probably was only in the water for two to three minutes before I heard you. Are you sure you didn't see or hear anything on your way to the stream?"

"No. Though I wasn't actively trying to catalog my

surroundings," he admitted. An idea Caleb didn't like pushed into his thoughts. He had to voice it. "I left the stream the way I came and you went out through there." He pointed toward the tree line closer to the stream that led back out to the trail's path. "There's a good chance our photographer was still there when we left."

Stress pulsed out from Nina like an electrical surge of energy. Suddenly Caleb was hyperaware of more than just her scent. The warmth of her skin radiated out to him, as if she was the flame of a candle. Licking out and taking the air around it. She tilted her chin down a fraction to run her eyes over the picture again. It brought her cheek even closer to his. In the fluorescent light her freckles took on a harsher contrast with her tanned skin. He suspected then that she had, at least in part, inherited her complexion and dark hair from a Hispanic parent. Her tan was too even, too rich, to be just from living in the sun. It made the shine of her lip gloss even more pronounced in contrast.

Caleb wondered how shiny felt before reality doused out the sudden curiosity.

"Whoever they were, they followed me."

Nina's voice had hollowed. Those shiny lips were downturned, sunken. Caleb returned his focus to the computer monitor.

She was right. Someone had either followed her to the trail or had already been on it before following her to the stream.

"There's also the possibility that they were already at the stream when you showed up and took advantage when you didn't see them," he said without much enthusiasm. "That would be one heck of a coincidence, I'll admit, but ruling out something just because it's unlikely isn't good practice either."

It sounded scripted because it was. Caleb had had the misfortune of being partnered with Neil Stewart before Jazz had moved to Overlook. He was a man who thought so squarely inside the box that, to him, even attempting to think outside of it was criminal. Caleb had told him over and over again to look from all angles and not just one. Neil hated the advice. To say the least, he and Caleb hadn't had the best of partnerships. The several complaints Neil had had filed against him for "conduct issues" had put a definite strain on them before Neil had finally transferred out of Overlook.

"But they sent an email to *me*," Nina said. "If they took the picture because of opportunity then they sure committed to making it personal really quickly." She pointed to the timestamp of the email. "I wasn't even back for an hour when it came in."

"There is that," he conceded. It didn't *feel* like a random, spur-of-the-moment thing. Still, that didn't mean it wasn't.

"It could have been a prank, too," he had to say. Nina scowled and he held up his hand to stop her from attacking. "I'm not saying it's a good one or one that should be taken lightly. But, as pretty as Overlook is, it's dreadfully boring for the younger demographic. One time Jesse Langford stole a surveyor's reel and a garden roller from the local hardware store and made crop circles out near the county line in Dresser's fields.

Because, as he claimed, there wasn't anything to do in town that got his blood pumping."

Nina stood tall, leaving only the smell of her shampoo to linger, and went around to the front of the desk. She balled her fists on the top of her hips.

"That email reads a lot more sinister than crop circles made by a bored teenager, don't you think?"

Caleb stood, still trying to show he wasn't trying to offend her or make light of the situation.

"I just meant that we don't know what this is yet." He grabbed his cowboy hat and held it against his chest. "But I promise you I'll find out. Okay?" Nina considered him a moment before nodding. "Now, I'm going to head out to the trail and see if our photographer isn't still out there. Are you doing anything in town today or hanging out here for a while?"

"I can stay here for now," she decided quickly.

Caleb nodded and put on his hat. He asked for her phone number and immediately called it. Nina saved his number.

"Call if you get another email or anything else happens that seems out of the ordinary. I'll come back by when I'm through."

Nina thanked him but before he could clear the doorway she called his name. Her eyes bore into his with a new intensity. Caleb was caught off guard once again.

"That's my work email for the Retreat. I've only used it for, and given it out to, shop owners and a few people around the ranch. It's not even on the website yet."

She didn't say anything more. Caleb didn't respond. They both already knew what that could mean.

Nina had already met whoever had taken her picture.

THE OFFICE DOOR remained shut and locked. Not that it made much of a difference if it were unlocked or even wide open. From the two large windows that sat behind her desk, she could see if any cars approached. Still, she felt better for throwing the deadbolt as soon as Caleb had left. The mysterious photographer hadn't had a car outside of the trail that she'd seen when she'd first arrived. He hadn't needed it to do what he'd done.

To spy on her, to take advantage of what she would have sworn was a private moment.

The email stayed open on her computer but she didn't want to use it. Not until this person was caught. Instead, she spent the time between Caleb's departure and when she could see his truck kicking up dirt along the road when he returned trying to stay on task. She double-checked events the town had going on through the next half year as well as notes for suggested events for the Retreat. They were already booked through the first month but she didn't want a slump in reservations soon after.

The need to succeed pulled at the center of her gut.

She wanted to help put the Wild Iris Retreat on the map. Even if she'd rather spend her life beneath that same radar.

Caleb parked out front and took a second to finish up the call he was on. He leaned against his truck, cowboy hat in line with the angle of his head tilt, brow drawn in and a frown darkening his expression.

He was a relative stranger to Nina. She'd caught him at the stream. He'd admitted to knowing the area and the trail by heart. Knowing where she worked and getting access to her email address would have been easy and more than plausible.

And yet...

Nina had believed him.

He wasn't the person who had taken her picture and, what's more, he'd been just as surprised at the email as she had been. Angry, too.

She bit the bottom of her lip in thought, watching his concern through the window. Caleb had certainly been a different kind of surprise, that was for sure.

He was handsome. There was no doubt about that. A cowboy who wore the title of detective well. Imagining him sitting behind a computer or sleuthing through a crime scene with a gun at his hip and a badge at his belt was as easy as picturing him out in the fields with the horses or down at the docks with a fishing pole. It was an interesting dynamic Nina hadn't thought to put together.

Though it certainly fit the attractive, strong-jawed man currently concentrating on a conversation she couldn't hear.

It was almost a pity when he finished it and headed to the Retreat's front door, ending the small show he'd unwittingly been giving her.

"I didn't find any clues other than some footprints and broken twigs and disturbed ground near the stream." He greeted her as she opened the office door wide. Caleb had already pulled his hat off and had it tucked against the side of his leg. "Whoever they were, once they got back onto the main trail I lost them."

Nina rolled her bottom lip over her teeth. She didn't know which she preferred, no clues at all or inconclusive ones.

"Don't worry," he continued. "I'm not going to just let this go away. Do you mind if I get on your computer to look up the IP address of the email that was sent?"

Nina didn't mind in the least. She waved him toward the desk and stepped aside. Beads of sweat ran along his neck. It seemed like morning had turned into late afternoon in the blink of an eye. A hot one, too, by the looks of it.

"Could you also make a list of everyone you've given your email address to?"

"I'm not the greatest with names yet," she admitted, a bit of heat pooling in her cheeks. "But those I can't remember I'm sure I could point out."

He fell into the office chair, eyes already narrowing in on the email.

"That works out fine. I can just fill in the blanks," he said offhandedly. "Overlook is a small town. Everyone knows everyone."

Nina decided to hold her tongue about the likelihood that someone he knew had no problem spying on women and got to work. It was a tedious task trying to remember the many faces she'd smiled politely at and hands she'd shaken. If only she had been more detail oriented—or, at the very least, invested in creating more than just business relationships—she wouldn't have had so many question marks in lieu of first names and surnames.

But she did. Something she apologized about when, after he was done with the computer, Caleb finally finished his second call outside the office.

"You do know you're in customer service, right?" he asked, eyebrow raised and a small smirk turning up the corners of his lips. "Usually that means remembering names."

Nina resisted the urge to place her hands on her hips.

"Our introductions were brief," she defended herself. "I just needed to know the basics and say hello. Then, at the grand opening party, I was going to spend more time getting to know everyone. I just didn't have the time to do that yet." It wasn't that much of a lie. Nina knew she'd have to play nice at the grand opening event Dorothy was throwing for the locals and the employees on the ranch.

Caleb snorted but didn't press. He folded the paper and put it in his pocket.

"Well, I'll look into the few names you have here and tomorrow we can try to hit up the rest in person. I have a buddy looking into where the email came from until then. He said he can give me an answer tonight or early tomorrow. Does that work for you?"

Nina nodded.

The sky outside of the window was darkening. A feeling of unease started to clench at her chest. Caleb's expression softened.

"Hey, it's been a weird day," he said, voice light. "I

haven't eaten since breakfast and, well, we got off on a really strange foot. I'm going up to Mom's for dinner. Why don't you come along? That woman doesn't make a meal you can't take seconds and thirds worth of leftovers home with you, so there will be more than enough."

He smiled. It made the handsome man even more so. Even his eyes, brilliantly blue, held an easy charm.

Her feeling of unease transformed into something else. An ache that was familiar yet just as raw as it had been the day, years ago, she realized her life would never be the same again. Like a switch had been flipped, Nina felt herself shutting down.

"I haven't even been here for a week and I got caught basically skinny-dipping," she said, voice hard. "I think it's best I focus on my work, if your mother decides to keep me around after all of this. I've already lost most of the day." When she wasn't sure if he was getting the point she was trying to drive home, she added, "I'll eat here. Alone."

Caleb's smile faded, but once again, he didn't press.

"I'll see you tomorrow then."

Nina didn't watch him go. Instead, she locked the door and walked up to her room. The familiar ache became a bellow in her chest. She sat on the edge of her bed and looked out of the window. In the distance the curve of the mountains held a beauty that did nothing to dissuade the memories about to overwhelm her.

Nina watched darkness veil the field and trees.

It would come for her heart next.

Chapter Four

The Wildman County Sheriff's Department was in need of a paint job. For whatever reason, the previous sheriff had painted the once copper- and red-toned bricks light blue. Since then the weather had changed that to a worn and chipped muck gray. Forget a happy-looking place, the one-story building now looked like a depressed cloud. And that was on its good days.

Yet peeling paint couldn't squelch the pride Caleb had in the department and the work he and his brother had done during their time there. He still felt it the next morning when he began his day. His metal desk with a perpetual stack of papers in the out tray, a framed candid picture of him and his siblings and the one empty coffee cup that always rested on a coaster felt as much of a home to him as the ranch.

Even on mornings where frustration clung to him like a second skin.

"Hodge said he'd call as soon as he was done talking to his boss," Jazz reminded him from over the tops of their desks. The fronts were pushed together leaving no space between. It made working together easier than having to hunt each other down. She didn't look up from the paperwork she was filling out as she continued. "I know patience isn't always your strong suit but that's what you're going to have to wear until he calls."

Caleb pulled out a stress ball Madeline had given him when he'd been promoted to detective. He squeezed it once, hard.

"Would *you* practice patience if some creep had sent that email to you?" He shook his head, answering for her. "You should have seen her, Jazz. It scared her and it happened on *my* land."

Jazz paused, her pen midword. She sighed.

"Just because someone sleazy did a sleazy thing on the ranch doesn't mean it's your fault," she said. "It's the fault of the sleazy person. Plus, you're trying to help catch that very same sleazy person. That counts for something."

Caleb snorted.

"You just said sleazy four times."

Jazz shrugged.

"If the shoe fits."

She went back to the paperwork. Caleb glanced at the clock above the closed door of the sheriff's office. Declan wasn't in and probably wouldn't be until they knew if there was an arsonist running through town. Caleb had decided to keep the incident with Nina under wraps for the time being. Partly because he could handle it, thanks to having no actively open cases, and partly because of Nina.

He had no doubt that his mother wouldn't have given the woman any grief over what had happened. Almost everyone at the ranch had, at one point or another, used one of the ponds or streams to cool down after a long day of work or exercise. That was nothing to be ashamed of, definitely not to be punished for. Yet the way Nina's words had hardened as she declined his offer to eat at the main house the night before had made him feel oddly protective. Not just of her physically, either. With a start, Caleb realized he wanted to help alleviate the embarrassment and worry that had colored her cheeks rosy.

He wanted to keep her safe.

He wanted to make sure she *felt* it, too.

"What about that list of people she gave you yesterday?" Jazz continued, pen moving across her paper. "Did you finish going through it?"

Caleb put the stress ball down and eyed the list in question. There was an X next to each name.

"Yeah. I talked to everyone she could remember the names of already this morning. Everyone had a solid alibi."

"Did you tell them what was going on with Nina or did you use that Nash family charm I keep hearing about to trick them into talking?"

Caleb chuckled. Jazz was trying to keep him busy, he knew, but she'd been giving him grief about the so-called Nash family charm since she'd moved to Overlook. She never saw it, she'd said time and time again. To be honest, neither did he, but that hadn't stopped the women in town from bringing it up to each other.

"Since I view you as a brother, does that mean I'm a part of that family charm, too?" she'd asked one day.

Caleb had chuckled then, as well.

"You know how small towns work by now, Jazz," he said. "All you have to do is say 'yes ma'am' and 'no sir,' and compliment their pecan squares."

Jazz snorted but didn't disagree. Caleb had gone back to squeezing his stress ball, distracting his hand from texting Hodge again, when his phone finally went off.

"Talk to me, Hodge," Caleb greeted him.

Hodge Anderson, the king of IT in town, answered in his usual gruff tone.

"Good news, bad news," he said. "Tracked the IP address to one location in Overlook."

"Bad news?"

"It's at Claire's Café."

Caleb grumbled. Claire's Café sold coffee, pastries and a small selection of books. It also had free wi-fi. It wasn't unusual for locals and out-of-towners alike to make the trek to Arbor Street with their laptops. Fast internet wasn't always easy to find in Overlook, and at the café it came with Claire's homemade pecan squares.

"Could you track it to the computer that sent it?" he asked, hopeful. Sometimes they couldn't get an exact location but just a general area.

"That *is* the bad news," Hodge persisted. "I think it's *Claire's* computer. It seems to be stationary, the best I can guess. It hasn't left the address in over a week."

Caleb felt his eyebrow rise, confusion pulling the strings.

"Are you sure?"

Hodge sighed.

"That's where the computer is that sent the email. You'll have to figure out the rest."

Caleb thanked the man before both said their goodbyes. He'd known Hodge since they were teens. Caleb questioning him had been more out of the need to be thorough. He trusted Hodge and his skills. However, that didn't mean he thought Claire Jenkins was the culprit behind the email. She'd been friends with his mother since *they* were teens. She didn't exactly strike him as the malicious type. Still, he put his stress ball back into its drawer and put his badge around his neck. He glanced at Declan's closed office door and then was in his truck, pointed toward the heart of town.

THE AIR WAS cool and the breeze was gentle. There wasn't the smell of salt water from the sea clinging to it like her childhood home, but the freshly mowed grass and the promise of rain was still a nice tradeoff. Nina picked her way along the manicured trail that led to the stables, trying to savor the charm of the ranch while pretending she wasn't tired to the bone. Falling asleep had been hard. Once she'd managed it, it had been restless. When Molly had shown up that morning, eager to run a fine-tooth comb over every inch of the cabins, Nina had welcomed the distraction.

Now that it was almost lunch, she decided that she didn't want to be alone just yet and took up Molly's offer to show her the horses. The manager, like most of the employees on the ranch, had soft spots for them. Because of this, Nina didn't mention that the last time she'd ridden had been when she was ten…and that she'd been terrified every minute of it.

"I hope this rain business keeps well enough away when we open," Molly said, clipboard checklist for the cabins beneath one arm. Her blond hair was braided tightly against her scalp. She'd left her cowboy hat in the office. Nina knew she'd need to get one soon. She needed to help sell the idea of a ranch getaway. She needed to look like she belonged and buying a Stetson seemed to be the easiest way.

"If it does end up raining, what do you think about taking the guests out to the barn near the trails?" Nina thought out loud. "Dorothy said it was once used for storage but is now empty, right? Maybe we could set something up in there to make them still feel like they're getting a camping or outdoorsy-type of experience without getting soaked. Maybe set it up to look like a makeshift campsite. Just a bit more comfortable."

Molly's brow scrunched in thought but her lips pulled up into a smile.

"You know, that could work," she said. "We could put in lanterns and decorate the barn like one of those old Western town attractions. I have to meet with Dorothy this afternoon. I'll run it by her and see if we can't go ahead and start working on the backup plan tomorrow."

Nina felt a swell of pride.

"I'll see if I can't come up with some activities, too. Maybe I can arrange something in town with one of the bars." As soon as she said it Nina's stomach clenched.

She had spent the night going over every person

she had given her email address to but still couldn't pinpoint anyone who had seemed *off*. Her gut hadn't yelled or even whispered through meeting or talking with the locals. No red flags, no strange behavior. Yet that email was still in her inbox, taunting her.

Nina had decided not to bring it up with Molly or anyone on the ranch. Not when Caleb already knew. She was sure it was only a matter of time before the news was out and she was let go for being so careless. That had been half the reason sleep had evaded her for so long the night before. Between the memories she had tried to leave behind to the very real possibility that she'd have to move back to her childhood home and live with those same memories again had almost put her in a cold sweat.

This had been her best chance at moving on. Starting over. Yet less than a month had gone by and her fresh start was being soured.

"That's a good idea," Molly responded, unaware that Nina had fallen back into a seemingly unending loop of memories and fears. "You should talk to the Nash triplets. They've spent their lives on this ranch. I bet they know how to keep entertained during every season around here."

"I can't imagine having triplets," Nina confessed, thankful for the slight distraction from her darker thoughts.

Molly laughed.

"Amen. Poor Dorothy has only been pregnant twice and yet has four children. Have you met any of them yet?"

Nina didn't want to lie as much as she didn't want to talk about the email. She nodded and went with a vague in-between response.

"I've only met Caleb, briefly."

Molly lifted up four fingers and ticked them off as she began.

"We have the eldest, Declan, who's the sheriff. He lives on the ranch in a house that used to belong to Dorothy's in-laws before they passed. He's a nice man but lets his work consume him. Which I guess you have to if you want to keep your community safe."

"Dorothy mentioned him. She said I wouldn't have to worry about any flak for throwing large scale events from local law enforcement since her son was the sheriff."

"A definite perk! Though, let me tell you, he's an intense fellow but it's just his way." Molly held up three fingers. "Then we have the triplets. Desmond, Caleb and Madeline. The only triplets born in Overlook in seventy years." Her smile disappeared. Her humor fell away. It was such an abrupt change that Nina wondered if they should stop their walk. But, just as quickly, Molly reverted to normal. "Desmond is a businessman, as best as I can describe him. He lives here on the ranch in a house built right behind the main one. He has a bit of money beneath his belt that he's made outside of the ranch. He's usually out of town on some work trip or another. Madeline lives there, too, since he's hardly ever home. She works with him, but last I heard she was trying to find something else to do. Then there's Caleb."

Obvious affection threaded around the detective's name. It prompted a flutter in Nina's stomach.

"I know you've already met him but, as a local gal, let me be the first to tell you that he spelled trouble when we were younger. Kids are kids, sure, but Caleb was an absolute wild child. Fearless. I was better friends with Declan yet I still have several stories of Caleb being a little daredevil." That change passed across Molly again. It was like the air deflated from her words. This time the change was slower to leave. "He's a detective now, one of the best Overlook has had, if you ask me. He lives on the ranch, too, in a cabin the triplets started to build after their father died."

Nina thought of the cabin she'd seen the day before with new attention. She didn't interrupt to say she'd already seen where the man lived.

A wistful smile lifted the corner of Molly's lips. "I once thought it was a bunch of bull-hockey that twins and triplets had a different kind of bond between them than other siblings—I mean, I have a sister who's my best friend—but once you see them together you'll understand it to be true. Maybe it's just genetics or maybe it's what they went through back in the day, but either way, once you meet the Nash triplets, you don't forget them easily."

They were getting closer to the stables. Nina could make out Molly's husband, Clive, with a beautiful almost-silver white horse in a pen. He waved at them, cowboy hat in his hand. Molly returned it with a wide smile. An ache of loneliness joined the ache from last night still radiating through Nina. Still, she didn't want the conversation to end.

"What they went through back in the day?" Nina repeated.

Molly gave her a sheepish look.

"I didn't mean to bring it up," she hurried. "It's just one of those things that I assume everyone in town knows." A haunted feeling crept over Nina. It pulled at the hair on the back of her neck. "When the triplets were eight someone abducted them from a park in town." Nina felt her eyes widen. She stifled a gasp. "That triplet connection they have saved their lives, at least that's how it was told to me by my mom when I was older. They were held for three days. Three. Can you believe that? Then, by the grace of God, they helped each other escape. Sure, they got hurt in the process, but all things considered it was a miracle. One the town still likes to talk about today, especially since the man who took them was never caught. And, believe you me, they looked for him for years." She shook her head. Her frown managed to pitch lower. "Honestly, since you're now employed by the Nash family, I'm sure someone in town will try to get more information out of you about it. Some insights they'd never heard before or, maybe, just some kind of theory they have about who was behind it. Still, it's not something the family likes to talk about so, please, keep it to yourself. The Nash family is a lot more than their tragedy."

"I won't say anything," Nina promised.

Molly gave her a polite nod. Her history lesson and rundown on the Nash siblings transitioned into talk about the stables and the horse Clive was with. It wasn't until Molly and her husband started talking about their daughter's latest homework assignment that Nina excused herself.

She walked along the side of the barn until she was at the wooden fence a hundred or so feet behind the stables. It encased a long-stretching field. A few horses were grazing in the distance, cresting along the curve of a hill. Nina watched them with admiration, and a small amount of dread. The last time she'd ridden a horse had been with her mother. She'd been terrified. Her mother had made her a promise.

"I won't let anything happen to you, Nina. Trust me."

Nina had still been terrified but nothing bad had happened. She'd been convinced her mother had worked some kind of magic. A spell.

Nina wished her mother had used that same magic on herself.

She placed her hands on the twisted wood of a fence post and took a long, deep breath. Caleb's face appeared in her mind as clearly as the green grass and gray, cloud-filled sky. She felt herself soften.

She often forgot that, just because she'd lived through something traumatic, didn't mean she was the only one who had.

Tragedy had a way of taking a person and changing their shape. Nina found herself wondering how it had affected one detective in particular but she finally came out of her thoughts enough to realize the cloud she'd been looking at in the distance wasn't a cloud at all.

It was smoke.

"Hey, Molly?" she called over her shoulder. Geography had never been Nina's strong suit in school but she was pretty sure the only building in that direction belonged to the same man she had been thinking about. Maybe they were doing a burn pile? But why there?

Nina ducked between two wooden posts and stepped out into the field. She glanced down at her watch.

Did Caleb take normal lunch breaks?

Was it her imagination or was the smoke cloud becoming larger?

Unease started to kick up in her stomach. Then Nina was running.

Chapter Five

No one was at the Retreat or the main office. Caleb thought about calling Nina since she'd given him her number the day before but decided to try the stables first. He didn't mind stretching his legs anyhow, especially since he was starting to get that mid-afternoon drag. He'd skipped eating lunch in lieu of going to Claire's Café.

Which was the reason he wanted to talk to Nina.

One of the reasons.

The other wasn't based in facts but feelings. He wanted to check on the woman, to make sure she was okay. As little contact as they'd had in the last twenty-four hours, she'd still managed to make an impression. One that passed itself on to Jazz. She'd offered to finish off the paperwork on their last case while Caleb figured out who was behind the email.

The walk to the stables was nice. It would rain soon. There was something inspiring about the charge in the air before a storm. Like everything around him was building up to something powerful. It put a little pep in his step, a little more focus in his gaze. For the first time since seeing Nina at the stream, Caleb wondered if she liked the ranch. She'd said she was from Florida, living on the coast.

He tried to remember what his mother had said after she'd interviewed and then hired Nina. She wasn't married, he knew that. No kids either. She had a business degree, but the specifics and where she'd gotten it, he didn't know. Like Caleb's ex had pointed out, he fell down the rabbit hole of work quite often. Sometimes when he'd resurface he was faced with a world that had passed him by.

That used to bother him when he was younger but now he was used to it.

Yet he couldn't help one surprising fact. He wanted to know more about Nina.

The stables were housed in an old tried-and-true weathered red building. It held twelve box stalls plus an office that Clive kept, a small room for the farrier and vet to use when they made their rounds and an attic loft overhead. Caleb was fond of that loft. The Nash siblings had each spent their fair share of time sneaking out of the house and congregating there with their friends growing up. Admittedly, it had been a while since he'd been there, but Caleb couldn't help but smile as he padded in through the tall, open front doors.

Clive was standing on the opposite end, finishing tacking up another reason for Caleb to smile.

"Well, if that isn't the most handsome stud I ever did see," Caleb exclaimed. Clive finished adjusting his horse's girth and then gently tugged on the saddle. He gave a good-natured laugh.

"Don't let Molly hear you calling me handsome like that," he said. "She might go and get jealous."

Caleb patted his friend on the back and focused on the horse staring at him.

"Been a while hasn't it, Ax?" he whispered, running a hand up and then down the side of Ax's neck. He was a frame overo Tennessee Walker. As beautiful as they came. Like Caleb could navigate the ranch with his eyes closed, he could perfectly imagine every white patch across Ax's dark copper hair without looking. The horse had been born on the ranch, just as Caleb had been.

"I was going to take him for some exercise," Clive said, taking down the tacking ropes. "The forecast said there was a good chance we'd be getting storms tonight and through the next few days. Thought I'd take him along the fence to make sure everything is on the up-and-up."

This wasn't anything new; once a week someone checked the fences. It was as much for keeping out predators and ill-willed humans as it was keeping the horses and livestock in and safe. Though the mightiest of fences didn't keep everyone out, especially if they were in tip-top shape. Case in point, the person who'd sent the email to Nina.

"I'm on my lunch break right now. If you don't mind the company I can tag along." Caleb patted Ax's head. The horse nudged into him.

"Sounds good to me," Clive said. "I can take out Isla—"

"*Clive!*" Molly skidded into the stables, eyes wild

and cheeks flushed. She looked between them as her chest heaved up and down. "I looked for Nina after she yelled for me but—but she's running through the field. There's smoke in the distance. Caleb, I think it's your house!"

Caleb didn't waste any time. His fingers wrapped around Ax's reins.

"Time to run."

THE AIR TOOK on the distinct smell that came with something large burning. It only propelled Nina forward with more urgency. What could she really do if the detective's house was the reason that smoke was climbing against a darkening sky?

Nina guessed cutting across the field at her fastest run would put her there before Clive and Molly could get there in the car. Maybe in that time she could do some good? Make sure no one was inside? Try and put it out herself until real help came?

Nina's lungs started to ache as she pushed up and over the top of the hill. The free-roaming horses had already run closer to the barn, not liking her frantic energy. She didn't blame them. As soon as she crested the hill she let out a strangled cry. She hadn't misremembered. The cabin in the distance was Caleb's. Though it was a lot farther away than she had thought, there was no denying that was what was burning.

Nina couldn't see the dirt driveway from her current angle. She couldn't tell if the truck was there or not. It renewed her drive to keep pushing. Her feet dug into dirt and grass harder, her legs took the force with a strained ache.

She couldn't stop. Flames were greedy. Lost seconds meant everything. She had found that out the hard way at the heartbreakingly high price of her mother.

A different kind of ache twisted within her so hard Nina almost stumbled.

I can't do this right now, she thought with decided concentration. *I can't think about her. Not when he could be in—*

Nina's thoughts were interrupted by the sound of hooves beating out a thunderous rhythm behind her. It wasn't until she felt them in the ground that she turned, worried the horses had been spooked even more and were about to trample her in their mad dash to escape.

What Nina saw brought her to a stumbling halt.

None other than Caleb Nash was charging toward her on horseback, detective's badge swinging on a chain around his neck and cowboy hat firmly on his head. Up until then Nina had never really gotten the appeal of cowboys, in the movies or real life, but right then she finally understood the allure. There was just something to be said about a man blazing across the earth with power beneath him and fire in his eyes. Yeah, she understood now.

Caleb was exactly where he belonged, sitting astride one of the most beautiful horses Nina had ever seen with an ease that somehow added to his appeal. When he stopped right next to her, Nina said the first thing that came to her mind.

"I-I thought you might be inside."

Caleb leaned over and outstretched his hand.

"Get on," he replied, voice all baritone.

It was all Nina needed to hear. She took his hand, put her foot in the stirrup, and let the man and momentum do the rest. It wasn't until her backside hit the saddle and her arms were firmly around the detective's stomach that Nina thought about her fear of horses. But then it was too late. They were cutting through the rest of the field with speed. The movement was jostling—she'd definitely feel it in the morning—but Nina clutched the man at the reins, trying to focus on anything other than the fence they were coming up on way too fast.

Was he going to stop or—?

Nina tucked her head against Caleb's back and squeezed her eyes shut.

"Hold on," he yelled into the wind. Like she wasn't already doing just that.

Nina felt the cowboy readying for the jump before the horse had even lifted off the ground. She clung to Caleb, focusing on the hardness of his chest and stomach instead of the fact that for one terrifying moment they were in the air. It wasn't until they hit the ground on the other side of the fence and ran a few feet that Nina loosened her death grip a fraction.

She heard the fire before she opened her eyes to see it.

Flames licked the left side of the cabin. From the porch to the roof, red and orange and black swirled together. The fire crackled and roared as it ate up the wood. Glass shattered as the heat hit the window, just out of reach of the flames. Caleb's body hardened within her arms. He brought the horse to a stop several yards out at the road. Nina held on as he swung his foot over and jumped to the ground. Wordlessly, he reached up and brought her down.

He handed her the reins, his face impassive.

"Stay here," he ordered, already turning.

"But you can't—"

He didn't give her the chance to argue. Caleb ran up to the porch and swung around it in the opposite direction of the fire. He disappeared around the corner.

Nina realized her heart was in her throat. The fire was consuming one side of the house but it wouldn't be long before it was destroying all of it. Movement flashed in front of the window next to the front door. She clutched the reins. Why had he gone inside?

A loud crack split the air. The left side of the house shuddered. Flames spiked higher in the air as half of the roof crumbled.

"Caleb!"

Nina dropped the reins, hoping the horse wouldn't go too far if he got spooked, and ran around to the house. The back door was wide open. Smoke had already filled the inside.

"Caleb." She tried again, taking an uncertain step forward. She couldn't hear anything else over the fire burrowing into the structure. No one moved.

Terror clawed at Nina's heart. Then she thought about her mom.

Only one person had been able to help when Marion Drake had been trapped. He had felt the heat, choked on the smoke, but decided not to move. He had watched instead, dooming her mother to a fate she hadn't deserved.

Nina didn't know Caleb. Not in any conventional sense, at least. They weren't friends or lovers. She hadn't grown up in town. She didn't know his middle name and he didn't know that she was allergic to scented fabric softener. She had no idea if he was single; he had no idea that she had broken up with her last boyfriend because he'd wanted to marry her. He wore a cowboy hat and a badge; she hid behind a wall of fallout left over from the trial of her mother's killer.

Yet it didn't matter.

Bolstered by thoughts of her mother and two of the bluest eyes she'd seen, Nina covered her mouth and nose with her arm and ran into the cabin.

CALEB DIDN'T MAKE it into his bedroom before the ceiling over it collapsed. He *did*, however, make it into the hallway that led there. The house seemed to moan and exhale all at once, unable to fight the pain that the fire was causing. He didn't have the time to watch through the open door as most of his belongings were crushed by weakened and burned wood. Instead he had to ensure he wasn't the one crushed next.

He retreated to the next open door. He didn't use it often but the office was still a room he hoped not to lose. At this rate though, he wasn't sure it stood a chance. All he could do was get out of the house and hope the fire department was speeding in their direction after Clive called. Caleb didn't have the time to puzzle out what could have started the fire but he wasn't an idiot. He knew they were past the point of using the water hose or an extinguisher.

Now the house was on borrowed time.

Just like him.

Caleb spun on his heel as he cleared the office door. He unintentionally sucked in a breath as the small hallway filled with debris. His lungs filled with smoke. It nearly doubled him over as a coughing fit took hold. The house shuddered again.

He moved to the middle of the room, trying to recover.

The only reason he'd come into the cabin in the first place was to make sure his mother wasn't inside. Like the pop-up surprise of spring cleaning, it wasn't unheard of for her to walk from the main house to his or Declan's and let herself in. She called it loving visits from the woman who'd raised them. Caleb called it her ninja training since she was always so sneaky about them.

Which was why he'd been terrified she had somehow started, and then become trapped by, the fire ravaging his home. He'd run into the house yelling for her, relief only partially coming through when no one has responded and he'd seen each room was empty.

Now that he knew she wasn't inside, his focus needed to shift to escape.

The window looked out to the wraparound porch and the field just beyond. He hurried over to it. He kept it open almost every time he used the office, preferring the smell of grass and daylight over the stuffiness of being confined, and it had a perfect track record for easily flipping open. Caleb pushed up on the glass. This time it wasn't easy. The window didn't budge.

Caleb coughed into his arm before he could zero in on what was making the window stick. His eyes were watering something fierce. It took him longer than it should have to figure out what he was looking at.

The windowsill was nailed to the frame.

From the outside.

The reflex to swear was only tamped down by another wave of coughing. The smoke had already been thick when Caleb had run in, now with the structure failing, it was undeniably worse. Never mind the coughing, it was getting hard to breathe.

Caleb backtracked to the armchair in front of his desk. It was what his sister had called a decorative chair, made to be pretty and not so much to be used. He'd thought that was silly but had obliged her. Now he was going to use the unnecessarily heavy piece of furniture to save his life.

He bent over to get purchase on the chair, hoping to use it like a battering ram, when he realized it wouldn't be that simple. He'd breathed in too much smoke. Now he couldn't breathe at all. Coughs racked his body. The house moaned again. Glass shattered. Something shifted.

He slumped against the side of the chair, trying to fight through the lightheadedness that bowled him over. All he had to do was pick the chair up and he'd—

"Caleb!"

The voice was competing with the fire but it was

undeniably there. Caleb turned around. Through watering eyes he saw two things back-to-back.

There was broken glass on his desk.

Nina was standing on the other side of the window, brandishing a shovel.

"Stand back," she yelled.

On reflex he turned his head. More glass shattered.

The urge to breathe twisted in his gut. Ached in his chest. Burned in his lungs. His head swam.

A hand grabbed his.

Even through the smoke Caleb was pulled into the dark brown eyes of Nina Drake. She'd not only broken away all of the glass, she'd come in after him too.

It was the shot of adrenaline he needed.

Caleb led her to the window but she pushed him through first. He climbed out onto the porch and took a stuttering breath, trying not to pass out. He waited until she was at his side, tucked Nina under his arm and together they ran straight into the field.

There Caleb's body decided it had been through enough. His knees buckled and they both went down. Nina did her best to catch them but only managed to put herself beneath him so she was on her backside with him on top. He tried to roll off onto the grass but she held him fast with one arm across his chest.

"You're—you're okay," she said, pushing up so that they were doing the best approximation of sitting they could manage. It took him a moment to realize she was propping him up, her chest against his back, her legs on either side of him. Something hard dug into his back but Caleb couldn't find the focus to wonder what it was.

Instead he let Nina hold him and together they watched as his home burned.

Chapter Six

The rain came next.

At first Nina didn't notice it. They just sat there, both trying to breathe again. The heat from the house traveled with ease. It didn't even seem possible that she'd ever feel the cold again. But then the darkness around them became hard to ignore. The smell of rain became the water that soaked into their clothes.

It wasn't until Clive and Molly came running around the house yelling that Nina even thought to move. Still, Clive was the one who got the ball rolling. He pulled Caleb to his feet and Molly helped Nina up. The four of them went back to Caleb's horse and then backtracked farther away from the house. Sirens came quickly after that. The sheriff was the first to arrive, beating them by a few minutes.

Declan Nash jumped out of his truck with his badge shining and his expression hard. He was a tall, solidly built man with a wholly intimidating disposition. When he saw his brother, however, every bit of him sagged with obvious relief. The rain rolled down both of their backs as they shared a heartfelt embrace. Nina kept her spot at Caleb's shoulder, silent.

They broke the brotherly hug with somber smiles. Both fizzled out quickly. Declan's voice was laced with disapproval.

"Were you inside? I thought you were with the horses when it happened."

The sheriff looked his little brother up and down, then glanced at Nina. She tried to remain impassive, not wanting to get any more grief thrown Caleb's way. Though she *was* curious about why he'd run inside. Then she felt the weight of what she'd taken from his office before leaving the house hidden beneath her shirt. No one had noticed the slight bulge. She'd wanted to give it to Caleb but until the sheriff had come flying down the road, the detective had been in fervent conversation with Clive and Molly. That conversation had concluded with both leaving, Clive on the horse named Ax and Molly in their car. Nina had decided to wait until she could have a moment alone with the man.

Caleb's voice had a rasp when he answered. The coughing fits had finally stopped but there was no denying he had been affected. Black smears from the smoke and ashes streaked across their clothes. The rain had washed most of it from their skin.

"I wanted to make sure Mom wasn't inside. You know how she wanders around here."

Declan's face softened. So did Nina. Caleb ran a hand through his hair, shucking off excess water. He'd lost his cowboy hat somewhere along the way.

"I got trapped in there," he continued. "Nina had

to bust out the office window with a shovel and come get me."

Nina flushed with surprise at the sudden attention. Declan raised an eyebrow. She shrugged.

"Anyone else would have done the same in my place," she said modestly. Declan flashed a quick smile.

One thing was for certain, the Nash sons sure knew how to own the simple gesture.

"Don't sell yourself short," he said. "It sounds like you saved the day."

Nina returned the smile. Then it was down to business.

"Declan, we need to talk about the fire," Caleb said.

There was a line of tension in him that seemed to tighten. He looked over his brother's shoulder. The fire had destroyed the office. The rain wasn't coming down hard enough to do any good. They'd been out there for over fifteen minutes and were just now hearing the sirens getting closer. "I don't think it was an accident," he continued. "The window in the office was nailed shut."

Declan reacted immediately. Rage burned behind his eyes. His fists balled.

Nina couldn't help the twist in her stomach. When she'd realized Caleb was trapped she'd run outside, hoping he had made it into the office before the hallway fell. That relief had been short-lived when she'd seen the nails embedded in the wood…and Caleb hunched over. Grabbing the shovel from the porch and using it to make an exit for him had been a blur.

"I was afraid of that." The sheriff swore. "I sent

Jazz to Mom's and told them both not to leave until we showed up."

"We need to make sure every place on this ranch is safe," Caleb said, determination warring with his rasp. "Molly and Clive have gone back to the stables to keep an eye on the horses."

"What about the Retreat?" Nina spoke up. It wasn't just a job, it was her new home.

"I'll make sure everything is okay," Declan told them both.

The fire department finally showed up, followed closely by an ambulance. Declan grabbed his brother's shoulder and looked him in the eye.

"This sucks," he said, simply. "But it's nothing we can't handle."

Caleb didn't nod but he didn't disagree, either.

The firefighters focused their attention on the fire while the EMT focused her attention on Caleb. She gave him oxygen and Nina a place to escape the rain. She sat on the bench along the wall in the back of the ambulance, watching with a feeling of detachment as the men and women tried to stop the flames. Not that it would matter much. Whatever wasn't touched by the fire was probably destroyed by smoke and water damage.

Caleb had undoubtedly lost his home.

Nina chanced a glance at the man. Sitting up on the gurney, he had an oxygen mask in one hand and a look of frustration on his face. The EMT shared that frustration. She spoke to him like a mother would a child.

"You need to come to the hospital," she tried. "Smoke inhalation can be serious, Caleb."

There was a familiarity in her words. Like most of Overlook, Nina bet she knew the Nash family personally.

"I'm fine, Linda," he said, still sounding hoarse. "I wasn't in there that long."

Linda shook her head.

"It doesn't matter. By the sound of it you took enough to almost pass out."

Caleb gave her a look that clearly said he was going to argue until he was blue in the face. Yet all Nina could see was the man in a room filled with smoke. She could still smell it on him. On herself. In the air, mingling with the rain.

She'd only ever seen the aftermath of what a fire like that could do.

If she hadn't come around to look for him, would he have made it out? Or would he have died like—

"Linda, listen," he started, his voice taking on the charming edge of a man who was used to getting his way with women.

Nina didn't know if it would work on Linda or not.

And she would never find out.

Something inside Nina shifted. She said exactly what was on her mind.

"My mom died from smoke inhalation. We should go to the hospital."

Caleb's blue, blue eyes widened. Nina felt a flush of embarrassment at being so blunt, not to mention personal, but stood her ground. "It's better to be safe than sorry."

Linda turned back to her patient expectantly. Caleb continued to look at Nina.

The rain picked up. It pounded against the roof in an unforgiving rhythm. The firefighters continued to yell back and forth in the distance, calling out orders as they became drenched. The fire was a constant, menacing roar.

Nina kept one arm over the small bulge in her shirt. Not that Caleb was looking anywhere other than her eyes. His stare was mesmerizing in its own right. She couldn't have looked away even if she'd wanted to.

Which she didn't.

She needed him to see what she was feeling. She needed him to understand the grief and anguish that still clung to her heart after all of these years. She needed him to take the trip that her mother had never gotten the chance to take.

She needed him to be okay.

And maybe he saw that in her. After a moment he nodded.

"Alright," he said. "Let's go."

OVERLOOK HAD A small but well-kept medical center on the south side of town. Nina had been surprised it had one but was grateful. The commute was short and the center wasn't crowded. They were led through a lobby that contained a handful of people before being sent back to a big room split into sections by faded green plastic curtains. Since she'd also been in the house, she was offered one of the sections while Caleb was given the one next to it.

Like most people, Nina wasn't a fan of hospitals. She eyed the bed and its paper covering with determination to not sit on either. The nurse promised she'd be right back before repeating the message to Caleb. She also seemed to know him. It made Nina feel like an outsider.

Which was good because that's what she had wanted.

To be seen and heard only when necessary.

To do her job with a smile and then go home, alone.

To live under the radar.

Not to get close to anyone.

A quiet life was better than the loud one she'd been forced into when she was younger.

The curtain next to her slid to the side. Caleb, still dripping wet, motioned to the space between their beds.

"Do you mind if we keep this open?" he asked. "I hate hospitals but I hate feeling cooped up in them even more."

Nina nodded, surprised that she instantly liked the idea despite just reminding herself that her desired lifestyle was keeping her head down. That was easier said than done, she was finding, especially when Caleb was the one looking at her. Like he wanted to say something more but the words seemed caught somewhere between his mind and his mouth.

"Yeah, sure. That's fine." She gave him a smile that echoed the sentiment. "I actually meant to give this to you outside of the house but, well, it was raining and I didn't want it to get messed up. Then the ambulance showed and, honestly, I got used to holding it and then forgot I was at all."

Nina pulled the picture frame from beneath her shirt. It was small and thin with chestnut-colored wood and a golden back. That's what had caught her eye in the first place. It was beautiful and compact, easy to carry. Though it was the picture encased inside that had made Nina decide to take it.

"I know it's not much in the grand scheme of things," she continued, holding the frame out. "But I know some things are a lot harder to replace than others."

Caleb took the frame but didn't speak right away. Nina worried she'd somehow misjudged the picture's importance to him, but then a smile pulled up the corners of his lips ever so slightly. He let out a small breath. The tension in his shoulders eased enough to show he was, at the very least, relieved.

"I was so focused on making sure Mom wasn't inside that I didn't even think to grab anything." He ran his thumb over the glass with affection. "This picture is one of a kind."

Warmth spread in Nina's chest at the admission. Caleb took a step closer and angled the frame so she could see the picture.

"This was taken when I was eight." He pointed at the eight-year-old version of himself. He was all smiles and blue eyes. On either side of him were a boy and girl who shared those blue eyes. "These are Madeline and Desmond," he explained before moving his finger along to a taller boy. "That's an almost-teenaged Declan, thinking he's hot stuff because he lucked out and got to kiss Corina Hoover during Spin the Bottle.

Believe me, I know, because he wouldn't shut up about it for *weeks*."

Nina stifled a laugh. His finger moved over to a younger Dorothy. Her hair was dark and long, her smile warm and inviting. "You've met Mom." Then Caleb pressed his finger against the image of the man holding Dorothy's hand. He looked so much like Caleb did now that Nina had no doubt it was his father. Still, she waited for him to say it.

"And this is my dad, Michael."

The smile that should have grown, faltered. Nina knew it well. No matter how many years went by, no matter how much she thought she'd moved on from her mother's death, there would always be those moments when the happy memories she had collided with the emptiness her loss left behind. Whether it was a smell of something familiar, a sound that stirred some forgotten story or simply a picture. It could make and break a child all at the same time.

Nina stepped closer and touched his shoulder.

"It's a beautiful picture."

Caleb nodded.

"It is."

Metal rings scraped along the curtain rod behind them. A woman Caleb seemed to recognize came in. She saw to Nina first. Caleb went back to his gurney.

He looked at the picture until it was his turn.

It HAD TAKEN Caleb an hour's worth of phone conversation to convince Desmond and Madeline not to hop on the next plane out of Texas and come back to the ranch.

He knew they were in the middle of securing a new investor that would mean a lot to their work. To leave would hurt their cause while showing up in Overlook wouldn't help solve the mystery. Caleb had had to use every excuse in the book as to why their flocking to him would only make things harder. The main reason being the simplest one.

He had a job to do.

While the fire investigator hadn't yet finished combing the aftermath of Caleb's house, he already knew what he'd say.

There was an arsonist in Overlook.

Caleb hated just thinking it, but the nails in the window were fairly damning evidence that the fire wasn't some freak accident. Someone had put them there before the fire.

Not only did he have a job to do in catching the culprit, he also had a ranch to protect.

And everyone who lived on it.

Caleb looked across the front porch of the Retreat's office at Nina. The rain was still falling but had lost its ferocity. Now it was a sound in the darkness of the night. A rhythmic backdrop to a day that had gone from relatively normal to hell.

After being cleared from the hospital, Caleb and Nina had been driven back to the ranch by one of the sheriff's deputies. Instead of going to the Retreat or the site of the fire, they were taxied to the main house. There waiting, sat his truck, his partner and his mother.

"Oh, Caleb," his mother had cried, pulling him into

an embrace. She repeated the sentiment with a partially contained sob.

"I'm okay, Mom," he'd consoled her. "It's just a house."

It was what his mother had needed to hear. She'd nodded then turned her attention to Nina. Word had already spread about her help and his mother had made sure the ranch's newest addition knew just how much she appreciated what Nina had done. They'd disappeared into the house together while Caleb had rendezvoused with Jazz outside.

She'd hugged him, offered up any and all help from herself and her husband, and then gotten down to business.

"Declan has a deputy at all of the properties not being watched by ranch employees tonight," she'd said. "Plus patrols around town. I don't know what he'll do tomorrow about it all, but at least tonight everyone here can hopefully sleep a little easier." She'd given him a pointed look at that.

"Don't worry," he'd said, picking up on the thought she wasn't voicing. "I'm not going to do anything crazy tonight."

It was true but only because there was nothing he really *could* do.

But he wasn't about to tell her that.

"Good. You need to get some rest. We can start figuring this out tomorrow," she'd promised.

They'd all convened in the kitchen for dinner. His mother was what his father used to call a nervous chef. When things went sideways, the cook- and bakeware came out. Together they'd eaten a late and extensive dinner. Jazz had helped his mother make a list of everything he might need while Caleb had fielded another call from each of his siblings. Nina had used the landline to make a call but had, for the most part, remained quiet.

Caleb hadn't forgotten what she'd said in the ambulance. Her mother had died from smoke inhalation. Which meant there had been a fire. The pain that had swept across her face as she said it hadn't been fresh. No. It had been old. Worn and felt over and over again until it had become the fabric of who she was. Caleb didn't need to know the specifics of what had happened to know the feeling.

And to guess how hard it must have been to go into the burning cabin.

Yet, she had.

He wanted to press, to understand how she was feeling, but decided to keep his distance. When and if she wanted to open up, he'd listen, but he wasn't about to push. He also knew how it felt to be prodded. To be watched. People waiting for him to break. He wasn't about to put that on the woman who had risked her life to save his.

Now, a few feet from where he stood wearing a borrowed pair of sweatpants two sizes too big and a jacket he'd found in a box in Madeline's old room, Nina held his stare with a sympathetic smile.

"I'm really sorry about your house," she said. "It *is* just a house but that doesn't mean it can't still hurt. Let me know if there's anything I can do."

"Helping me out of the burning building was more than enough," he replied. "But thank you."

He waited for her to unlock the Retreat's door and walked her to the office. Her purse and phone were still on the desk. Caleb checked the window to make sure it wasn't nailed shut while she went through her phone.

A feeling of shame washed across Caleb. With everything that had happened he had forgotten what he'd gone to the stables that morning to do in the first place.

"We tracked down the IP address from the email you received today. It led to Claire's Café in town," he recounted. "Have you been there before? It wasn't on the list you gave me."

Nina's eyes widened in recognition.

"I haven't been there yet but Molly and I ran into the manager at the grocery store." She gave him a sheepish look. "I couldn't remember her name. She talked mostly to Molly. Wait, *she* sent the email?"

Caleb shook his head.

"It traced back to the café, to Claire's office computer. She had no idea what I was talking about so we looked at the security footage and saw Daniel Covington pick the office's lock and sneak in there yesterday."

Nina's brow furrowed. By the looks of it she didn't seem to recognize the name. Which wasn't surprising.

"Daniel is a nineteen-year-old pain in the ass, to be blunt. We've had trouble with him in the past for taking pranks too far," Caleb continued. "He hasn't done something like *this* but he's sure going to answer for it. A uniform took him into custody just after lunch. Claire is pressing charges for the invasion of her privacy, plus breaking and entering. I assume you might want to, as well, considering the invasion of yours."

"I do," she agreed. "If only to make him think twice before trying this again."

Caleb nodded at that sentiment. The motion somehow felt exhausting all of a sudden. He ran a hand through his hair. His cowboy hat had fallen off when he was in the house. Just another piece of his life gone.

"Hey, Caleb?"

Nina's expression had gone impassive. Caleb could no more read her now than he could back at dinner. He took a step forward, though. There was something magnetic about the raven-haired woman.

"What happens now?"

It was such a simple question.

It only made sense to give it a simple answer.

He straightened his back and answered in a low yet clear voice.

"Now I'm going to catch whoever did this and stop them from doing it again."

Chapter Seven

The fire was ruled arson. Not even a particularly clever one, at that.

Residue from fireworks was found beneath what used to be Caleb's bed and all the windows had been nailed shut. They couldn't decide if that was meant to trap someone or to keep them out, considering the doors had not been tampered with. As for leads on the arsonist, Caleb and Jazz only had the fireworks to go on. There was a big chain store that sold them two cities away but there were also roadside stands that popped up on occasion. Even if there had only been one store, that didn't mean too much. They couldn't track down everyone who had purchased fireworks.

So Caleb had tossed around the idea that he was targeted because of his job—maybe someone he'd closed a case on or their kin was angry?—and had been working through that long list for alibis. He had also worked with the fire chief by getting information on all fires in Overlook in the last five years.

He wanted to be thorough.

Whoever the arsonist was had made it personal,

which only drove Caleb's heels harder into the dirt. The news had had varying effects on the other Nash family members.

Dorothy Nash was a force to be reckoned with. Her worry for her family and the ranch focused on Caleb. Convincing her that he was alright during the next week was almost as hard as skirting Jazz's and Declan's concerns. At least Desmond's and Madeline's calls and texts were more manageable. The only person who gave him any space to breathe was Nina.

Although he had holed up in Desmond's house since they would be in Texas for at least another week if not two, Caleb had made a deal with her the day after the fire. Since Declan couldn't keep deputies stationed outside every building on the ranch, Caleb had offered to keep an eye on the Retreat at night. Losing his home had hurt him, but losing the Retreat would hurt the family.

And then there was Nina.

She'd risked her life to help him. He'd do no less for her.

For the next week they fell into a routine. He would spend the night camped out on the office's couch and get up in the morning and head to Desmond's to shower and get ready for work. Then he'd be back by dinner and they'd repeat the routine. During that time Nina had been friendly and polite. They took turns handling dinner and breakfast, her inviting him up for something she'd made or his bringing something from the main house, and they'd even played a game of Scrabble one night. Sometimes Molly showed up for a few minutes and sometimes they didn't even speak.

It was comfortable. Nice, even.

Yet the longer their time together went on, the more Caleb started to realize Nina wasn't keeping to herself for his benefit.

No. It was for hers.

That's when he noticed the walls.

When she seemed to want to say something but would stop herself. The smiles she cut off before they grew too big. The way she quieted when he got too far out of the range of small talk.

Nina Drake was a guarded woman.

And it only made her more intriguing to him.

When Friday morning rolled around Caleb's curiosity finally bonded with this frustration over the case. He finished his coffee and set it down on the picnic table with purpose. Nina looked up from her half-filled cup and laptop. They were at the communal area between the Retreat's office and the first cabin, enjoying the sunshine that had been hit or miss the last few days. Caleb hadn't missed how it made Nina's hair shine, or how every freckle seemed to be highlighted beneath the light.

"Would you like a tour of the town?" he asked without any preamble. Nina's eyebrow arched high. "Well, less like a tour and more like being a fresh pair of eyes to places that previously burned to the ground."

If possible her eyebrow went higher.

"Sadly not the weirdest proposition I've gotten." She laughed. "Care to elaborate?"

Caleb tapped the printout he'd been looking over since he'd woken up.

"I'm trying to figure out a pattern to the fires that were ruled arson in the last few years, but I think I'm too close to them. Every place on this list I've been to, not only as an adult, but a kid. Maybe you can see something I'm missing."

Nina glanced toward the office. While it had been a pain, they had all decided that if the arsonist wasn't caught by Monday it would be best to cancel the reservations set for the following week. Never mind the grand opening party. Sure, it wouldn't be good for business, but having someone set fire to the guest cabins during their stay would be, without a doubt, worse.

"If I can help, I'm definitely in," she told him. "When do you want to leave?"

"I need to head up to Desmond's and then I'll be ready. Does that work for you?"

She nodded and took a long drink of her coffee. "I just need to let Molly know. There's not much else I can do here if we can't open the Retreat."

Caleb helped her clean up and then they went off in separate directions. It wasn't until he was out of the shower and putting on his boots that he realized the new excitement dancing around his gut wasn't just about potentially finding a lead.

NINA DIDN'T KNOW what one wore to an old crime scene so she opted for a black undershirt with an open, flannel button-up and a pair of Levi's she was proud to say had fit her for the last three years. She pulled her long hair back into a ponytail. Then she put on lip gloss.

That move surprised her. She almost took it off before the cream-and-brown striped truck she was getting used to seeing came to a stop just outside. Nina waved goodbye to Molly and tried to tamp down the sudden uptick in the speed of her heartbeat. She'd spent the last week with the man, more or less, and had been fine. Changing locations shouldn't make a difference.

The inside of the truck cab smelled of men's cologne and the woods, both wrapped into one surprisingly intoxicating scent. It made Nina's heart beat a little bit faster against her chest. She gave Caleb a polite smile, hoping to cover up the new feeling.

"So, these are the places in the last five years that have had fires that did a good amount of structural damage," he told her. Nina took the paper from him as they started out to the road that led out of the ranch. There were five addresses.

"Were all of these arson?"

Overlook was small. Five acts of arson in the last five years was shocking.

"No. Only two were ruled arson," he explained. "The other three were caused by human error. Accidents. The first on the list is the earliest one."

They drove out to a large middle school, two minutes from Overlook's main thoroughfare. It was one of the few stretches of land outside of the ranch that wasn't surrounded by fields of grass or trees. Instead it was boxed in by houses. Caleb drove to a house on the other side of the fenced-in schoolyard. He parked and pointed through the windshield to the two-story house. There was a wooden For Rent sign staked in the yard.

"The fire started in the bedroom and destroyed the entire house. The owner, Angelica DeMarko, fell asleep watching TV and woke up to flames. She said she had no idea how it started, but an investigation showed she fell asleep with a lit cigarette in her hand, dropped it and it caught the curtain next to the bed on fire. From there it made it to the closet where she kept some camping supplies, including kerosene. The fire became much more violent before the fire department could even get there. She was lucky to wake up when she did and get her and her kid out." They got out of the truck and walked up to the house.

"Is this any of the old house?" she asked, admiring the wood and stone porch columns. Nina had always been a fan of the rustic style.

"No, the original had to be demolished. DeMarko didn't have insurance so the land ended up going to the bank and the bank sold it to a man who rebuilt and made it a rental property. Only one family has rented it since but then moved. I think because of a new job opportunity for the mother."

Nina walked around the house before coming to a stop at Caleb's side. He was staring at the school play-ground. A wistful, almost vulnerable smile graced his lips. Nina felt like she was intruding on a memory. She started with an apology.

"I'm sorry but I don't know exactly what I'm look-ing out for," she admitted. "If there's a connection to the fire on the ranch, I'm not seeing one here."

Caleb nodded, not at all nonplussed.

"I thought the same when I came out here earlier this week. But I'm glad for an outsider's point of view to back it up."

Nina felt a small sting at him calling her an outsider, even if it was exactly what she had wanted when coming to Overlook in the first place. Caleb let out a long exhale but kept his gaze on the playground.

"I went to Overlook Middle," he started. "All the Nash kids did. You see the monkey bars over there? For as long as I live I'll never forget when Madi punched Nico Meyers right where the sun don't shine when he was trying to swing across." He chuckled. It pushed his smile wider.

"Did Nico deserve it?" Nina ventured, curious despite herself.

Caleb shrugged.

"I wouldn't say that should be the penalty for doing a dead leg but that's exactly what he paid."

"A dead leg?"

Caleb gave her an incredulous look.

"You don't know what a dead leg is?" When she shook her head Caleb only became more amused. It was nice to see him smile so much, she decided. For good reason he'd been trapped in a constant state of seriousness. Their brief conversations over the last week had gotten a few smiles but none that reached his eyes.

And Nina should know, she'd spent more time than she should have staring at those beautiful blues.

"It'll be easier to show you instead of tell you. Do you mind?"

"I don't mind."

Caleb told her to stay still and moved behind her. Nina felt heat starting to crawl up her neck in anticipation. She tensed.

"I won't let you fall," he said. "Just trust me."

Before she could respond Caleb put his knee into the back of hers. The sudden pressure and surprise made her buckle. Two hands wrapped around her upper arms. They were warm and strong and stopped her descent with ease. The blush that had been stretching from her stomach to her cheeks finally reached its destination.

"*That's* a dead leg," Caleb concluded. He let go but the warmth of his hands still lingered. Nina turned to face him while also adding an extra step back for more distance. "Nico did that to Madi in the cafeteria in front of the entire sixth grade class, but more importantly her crush. She *and* her food tray hit the ground hard."

Nina tried to cover the sudden heat within her by laughing.

"Then I might have given Nico the same treatment," she decided.

"Mrs. McGinty wasn't as understanding." He moved back to her side and, together, they looked at the playground again. "She grabbed Madi's hand and marched her across the yard, yapping about her actions being unladylike." He snorted. "Madi told her it was unladylike to *not* stand up for herself."

"I like the sound of little kid Madi," Nina admitted.

"You'll have to tell her that when she gets back with Des." Caleb's smile burned bright once more. Then it fizzled out. "I can only convince them to stay away for so long."

A small silence settled between them. Nina didn't know what to do. Caleb was strolling down a more intimate conversational path than he had in the last week. Which meant it was only a matter of time before he tried for more personal details about her.

No sooner had she had the cringe-worthy thought than the question came from his mouth.

"Do you have any brothers or sisters?"

Caleb gave her an expectant look. Nina shook her head.

"I was what my father affectionately liked to call a 'happy surprise.' They had me when they were just twenty. At the time they barely could take care of me so they decided to wait before trying again." Nina traced the playground's slide with her eyes, careful not to give anything away. "My mom passed away before they could get there."

"I'm sorry, Nina."

She shrugged.

"It's okay. It happened a long time ago."

"Just because it happened a long time ago doesn't mean it's okay." Nina wanted to go back to the truck without another word but stilled her feet. The man's words had been too sincere to walk away from, especially since they rang true.

"I know," she agreed.

They went back to looking at the school in the distance. A new guilt emerged in the pit of Nina's stomach. Caleb and his siblings had been abducted and held for three days.

Had they hollowed him out?

Were his smiles and bright, blue eyes a show?

Or had he moved on?

Nina found a question forming on the tip of her tongue, wondering aloud how he managed to stay in a town filled with terrible memories, but then she thought of her mother and decided to give the man an answer to an unasked question.

"She was trapped inside of a burning car. My mother, that is," she said, perhaps with a little more bluntness than she intended. "I was told the smoke is what actually..." The words trailed off. They never came easy when on the topic of what happened.

Even when Nina wasn't telling the whole story.

Caleb waited for her to gather her thoughts. She did after a moment.

"Tragedy. That's what everyone in town called what happened, and then, in another breath it seemed they'd tell me that I would move past it one day. I would wake up knowing what had happened had and yet find the ache had lessened."

Nina chanced a sad smile at the man next to her. She pressed her hand to her chest.

"It's still there. After all these years, it's still there."

Caleb's face filled with an emotion Nina couldn't describe. He let out a small breath. His shoulders sagged slightly.

"Tragedy. Death. Trauma. I don't think it's supposed to go away," he said. "I think it only moves. Some days it's right next to you, staring you in the face. Others? It's all the way at the edge of your memory like a whisper. Like a bad dream." That unaccounted for emotion was replaced by the face of a man who had lived through his words. It made Nina want to dive into Caleb's past right then and there. Yet, again, she stilled herself from the impulse.

She knew the headline about the Nash triplets. She wasn't going to expect intimate information about his past that she wasn't willing to part with either.

"At the end of the day I think it just comes down to how fast we can wake up," he added.

It pulled out an unexpected smile from Nina. Caleb matched it before she'd explained its presence.

"That sounded wonderfully poetic," she admitted.

Caleb chuckled.

"Don't let the brains and brawn fool you," he said, jokingly. "I can also make pretty words."

And just like that the moment was over.

Nina went to the truck and Caleb followed.

Chapter Eight

The second fire had been caused by an unattended grill in the back of an at-the-time new restaurant on the main strip. Instead of stopping and walking around the building like they'd done with the last, Caleb pointed out the still-standing restaurant while stopped at a pedestrian crossing.

"They were quick on their feet and used an extinguisher to put the fire out," he said. "They lost a grill in the process but had no problem replacing it. The cook didn't even lose his job."

He took a left off Main Street. The road twisted and turned and then they were driving up an incline to two rows of houses. This time they stopped at the curb. Caleb pointed to a house with a bright yellow door. It reminded Nina of the beach houses she'd grown up around.

"This fire wasn't a fun one, not that any are," he started. "Gloria, the owner, left some candles burning while she went to the store. When she came back the living room was engulfed. Gloria's two dogs were still inside. She fought off her neighbors to go back in after them but passed out before she could get back out. Firefighters managed to rescue her but she had to spend a few weeks in recovery."

Something in Nina's memory sparked. "Is this the same Gloria who runs the nonprofit animal shelter?"

"The one and only." There was pride in his voice. "Gloria has been volunteering, and helping people and animals alike for as long as I can remember. Her and her ex-husband started a no-kill shelter in the next city over. She puts a lot of her own money into saving as many animals as she can. We even have a few from her organization out on the ranch."

"I remember reading about her when I was looking through old news stories in my search for local events. When did the fire happen?" Nina was trying to recall the date on the article but she'd looked through so many pieces since accepting the Retreat job that they all had blurred together.

"Two years ago," he answered, putting the truck in Drive again. "The town came together to help in any way we could. She was able to get repairs and still lives there. *With* her two dogs."

Nina couldn't help but smile at that.

They drove to the opposite side of town. Caleb rolled his window down. Nina did, too. The wind smelled like sunshine and sweetness. It tangled her hair but she didn't mind. Caleb turned the radio up and started to sing along with a song she didn't recognize. Nina was surprised at first, worried talk of fires would only plunge him back into a distant mood, but then she realized what must have been the key to Caleb Nash's happiness.

Sunshine.

It was such a warming thought that when he turned her way Nina gave him a genuine smile. There was something beautiful about a man who took delight in such simple pleasures. The same man who had admitted that the pain of trauma never really went away, it was just a matter of distance. It amazed Nina that Caleb could still seem whole after everything, even after the recent loss of everything he owned. His good mood was contagious and as they drove down a dirt road that cut through a field of green and grain, Nina felt the weight of worry lift from her shoulders. For a little bit they were just two people enjoying the country air, hair in the wind and the radio on.

But then that dirt road led to several BEWARE and DO NOT ENTER signs. The truck stopped. The windows went up. The radio cut off. Caleb's easy smile shut down. He didn't offer any preamble as he got out. Nina followed, her stomach knotting slightly.

The signs, plus traffic cones and a barrier, were standing sentry across the road, stopping any drivers from plowing straight over a drop-off and into dark blue water. On the other side of the water was the same collection of signs and warnings. Declan had already arranged for the debris to be cleared during the last week but there was still some that had sunk into the water.

"This is Overlook Pass. Locals usually come here for fishing since it's one of the deeper parts of the river." Caleb stopped just before the edge and motioned from one set of signs and then to the other. "The bridge that *used* to be here was given historic landmark status a few years back. Last week one of the sheriff's deputies realized it burned down."

There was a tightness to Caleb's voice. An anger igniting below the surface. His hand balled at his side. Nina felt the sudden urge to reach out to him. To let him know whatever was wrong would be okay. Yet she stilled herself and let him continue.

"It was ruled arson. They think kerosene was the accelerant but apparently the unknown timeline has thrown them for a small loop. No one knows when it actually happened yet since this spot isn't as popular this time of year. Plus it's far enough out of town that if the wind was blowing in the other direction, no one in town would have seen it."

Nina took one small step forward and looked down at the water. It wasn't the ocean but it still was pretty. When she turned back she saw a house in the distance.

"They didn't see when it happened? The people who live there?"

"No one has lived there since the owner moved out of state to live with her daughter." Another memory sparked in her mind but Nina couldn't catch it this time. "The last fire on the list is at a house a few minutes from here. It happened the day we met."

The house on Brookewood Drive landed a more impactful punch. It was one thing to look at the restored buildings and an empty space where the bridge had once been, it was another to see a beautiful home burned to its core. Caleb's tension was palpable as he stood at the curb.

Nina hadn't stepped away from the Retreat since the fire on the ranch. Molly hadn't either. Together they'd wordlessly been protecting it while Clive had done the same with the horses at the barn. Caleb had moved between his brother's house, his mother's house, the Retreat and work. Nina felt like an idiot for just realizing that circuit would, of course, have included at least once the remains of his own house.

Did it look like this? Was it recognizable or just a pile of debris and ashes?

Nina didn't think she could ask, though guilt welled up inside of her. She should have already talked to him about it.

"Kelso and Maria Gentry's neighbors called it in while the couple was in town," Caleb started. Nina came to a stop at his side. She couldn't help but stand close to him. The sight of the husk of a home was almost painful to look at. Part of the house had survived the flames but she doubted anything else had. "The investigator and lab found traces of kerosene. That plus the couple's new fancy furniture that had polyurethane foam padding, and everything burned fast. It was a miracle the fire department made it here when they did or everything would be gone."

"So, no fireworks then."

Caleb shook his head. Standing as close as she was Nina caught a wonderful, spicy smell that must have been lingering from his shampoo. It was, in one word, intoxicating. In another, inappropriate. She tried to refocus.

"This fire was started in the study." He pointed to the debris to the left of the still-standing portion. "Unlike my house, it was a room more in the heart of the house instead of outside. There's also no nails in the windows."

"Okay, so, other than them both being fires, they don't have anything else in common?"

"Not that I can tell."

"But surely two cases of arson in the same town within two days of each other, not to mention the bridge, aren't coincidences. Especially with traces of kerosene at two," she pointed out. "Right?"

In profile, Caleb's jaw hardened.

"Right."

They looked at the house for another minute or two before they were back in the truck and headed toward the ranch. Six fires in the last five years. Three accidental, three arson. Two different methods for those arsons. Kerosene and fireworks.

Were they all connected?

Or *were* they just a series of coincidences?

Was there an arsonist in Overlook setting random fires?

Or had Caleb been targeted?

Nina sighed. The distant curve of a mountain made her feel impossibly small. Just like she had the night her mother died.

"I'M SORRY."

Caleb put the truck in Park and gave Nina a look that revealed his confusion. The raven-haired beauty continued, eyes dropping away from his.

"If there are any connections or clues that could give you a lead, I'm still not seeing them."

Caleb shook his head.

"I wasn't expecting to show you these places and you have a magic answer to solve everything," he admitted. "I just wanted to make sure what you saw was in line with what I had."

He tightened one hand on the steering wheel and pulled his gaze away from the windshield ahead of him. Molly was outside one of the Retreat cabins, her laptop in hand. She kept her attention on it, giving them privacy.

"See, I love Overlook," Caleb continued. "I was born here, grew up here, and even though I left for school, I came back here. I know every road, every incline, every trail like the back of my hand. That almost goes the same for the people. That kid Madi punched on the playground? He's in the running to be the mayor. His sister, Bekah? She works at the library, though she didn't always. After her and her husband, Kevin, split because he was getting too friendly with Marla over at the flower nursery, she decided she wanted to get back to her roots of what she was passionate about. She loves to read, just like the other librarian, Lamar. His father wasn't happy he didn't join the military like his brother did, but they've since buried that old fight. Now you can find Lamar and his dad eating lunch together almost every day in town." Caleb glanced over at Nina. Her eyebrow was arched up in question. Why had he just babbled on about town gossip, he guessed she was wondering. He held up his index finger.

"That's just one, long connected thread that makes up this town. You give me a name and I bet dollars to donuts I can follow it through every person and home in Overlook. *That's* how well I know this place." He paused, trying to keep the flash of anger he felt from showing. "Which is why an arsonist showing up and doing what they did has thrown me off my game. Sure, there's people here who don't respect the law—we have our fair share of misconduct and violence like any town or city—but usually I can understand it and why the person did what they did. But this? Destroying the Gentry's home? Nailing windows shut so my place could burn without interruption? I can't even guess who it is. That's rarely happened to me before in this job and it's gnawing at my gut. Which is exactly what happened to Dad."

Saying it was like a jolt to his system. Caleb hadn't meant to say exactly what he was feeling. Not out loud, not to Nina. Yet there was something about her that made him feel comfortable. Or maybe it was his curiosity that had prompted the admission. How could he hope to know more about her if he never opened up about himself?

"He was a detective too," he explained. "A great one, but there was one case that ate him up. He didn't understand the why of it and he certainly never got any answers. The stress, well, it killed him."

Caleb wondered then if Nina knew about the abduction. He was so used to everyone already knowing about it that the possibility that she hadn't been told hadn't crossed his mind. It had been years since any of the Nash family had told the story themselves. It seemed to circulate just fine without them, making its way through the locals even all these years later.

But Nina wasn't local.

If she didn't know, now would be the perfect time to tell her. To open up to her even more.

However, an old resentment flared to life just beneath his skin. The child in him, the teenager, the young adult... They'd been questioned off and on throughout the years about those three days held captive. He'd been asked to tell the story more times than he could count, bombarded by curiosity that had no business being so curious.

He wanted to open up to Nina—after risking her life to save his, especially—but that resentment at sharing the single worst experience the Nash family had gone through kept the story buried. The weight of pain that pressed into his chest when he spoke again was only for his father.

"He thought he knew this town, these people, and yet he died with nothing but questions."

Caleb let out a long breath. He was back to the fires. Just like his father, he had so many questions. The most urgent ones being who and why.

Nina's hand pressed against his shoulder, surprising him. A small smile graced her lips. Her shining pink lips.

"Hoping that we know that our neighbors don't have bad intentions is like hoping no one ever acts on those bad intentions. If I've learned anything in my life, it's that people are people. They're complex, confusing, wonderful and terrifying. You can't beat yourself up because you don't understand why someone would do something bad. The best any of us can do is continue to struggle to understand. It just shows that we would never do the same things." She squeezed his arm. "The people who take from us shouldn't be allowed to keep taking from us. Don't beat yourself up because someone else finally showed their true colors. Okay?"

Caleb nodded, stunned.

"And I'm sorry about your father," she added, voice as soft as a feather.

"Thanks." He meant it.

Nina smiled a bit brighter and then dropped her hand.

"Will you be eating dinner here tonight?" she asked, opening the truck door.

"If that's okay with you."

"That works for me. Molly brought in some leftover stew today. There's plenty for the two of us." Her eyes turned sharp. Her smile faded. "You'll figure this out, Caleb. And I'll do my best to try and help you."

Caleb didn't get a chance to say thank you again. He watched as she walked away. The tightness in his chest lessened.

He drove back to Desmond's house and nodded to Roberto, the Retreat's cook, who was sitting on Dorothy's back porch on the phone. He'd been a lifelong friend of the Nashes and had offered to do his planning work at the main house to keep the Nash matriarch company. Caleb had no illusions that Declan hadn't helped with the arrangement. The department was being stretched thin at the moment. They needed to grab peace of mind where they could.

Desmond's house was a two-story farm house, with white shiplap, exposed wood and a tin roof that made the rain sound like a song that put Caleb to sleep every single time. It was a nice, solid house, but it wasn't Caleb's no matter how much he tried to ignore the reason he was there in the first place.

He bounded up the stairs and into the guest bedroom across from Madi's room. He'd gone through the ashes of his home, looking to salvage what was left. All that could be saved fit into a plastic container his mother had gotten from Walmart. It was shut and pushed into the corner. Caleb could still smell the smoke.

He fell down onto the edge of the bed. He needed to figure out who the arsonist was and fast. Yet the more he sat there, Caleb realized, the more his thoughts pulled away from him. As the afternoon darkened into night and every phone call and theory hit wall after wall, he finally looked at the only piece of his home that had escaped the fire and smoke unscathed. Thanks to Nina.

Caleb gently picked the framed picture up.

It had been a warm and happy spring. Dorothy and Michael Nash had been happy. So had their children. None of them had had any idea in the world what was going to happen next. The weight of worry, the burden of tragedy. The decline of a detective who couldn't solve the case that nearly cost him his family. No. Not yet. Instead they were frozen forever in a pure moment of happiness.

And Nina Drake had saved that just for him.

THE STEW WAS delicious and the night was beautiful. Nina enjoyed both alone. The cowboy detective apologized when he came in late to the Retreat before answering one of several calls that kept him at a distance. It bothered her, if Nina was being honest. She was starting to find that wanting to be alone wasn't as easy as she'd been pretending it was.

Though maybe that had more to do with the man with steel-blue eyes and an arresting jawline. Not to mention a quiet sweetness she hadn't expected after their first awkward meeting. She suspected that finding the person who had destroyed his home wasn't an act of vengeance but of concern. Concern for his family, the ranch that served as their livelihood, the town that was their community and her. Whether that was wishful thinking or not, Nina couldn't shake the feeling that something was changing between them.

She had meant what she'd said in the truck. When he had revealed how his father had passed away, she had seen the stress and pain pulling him down. Nina was also presumptuous in thinking she saw a struggle there too. A hesitation. The case that Caleb's father had tried to solve had to have been about the triplets' abduction.

Molly had said the man behind it was never caught. She could imagine how that might tear apart not only a detective, but a father, as well.

The realization that the abduction had eventually cost Caleb his father too had pulled Nina's personal experience with her mother's death to the forefront.

The car accident hadn't been an accident, yet she kept that detail to herself.

And she made sure to extend the same courtesy to the man who had been vigilant about keeping her safe.

Nina knew it was easier to keep quiet than relive your worst experience over again. She owed him that.

So, she waved goodnight to the detective and put all thoughts of him out of her mind as she showered and got ready for bed. She finally called her father, Trevor, and they spent almost an hour talking about his newest adventure with his wife, Denise. They'd been married for a little under a year but had been dating for three. Nina had grown to love Denise. It had been easy after seeing how happy she'd made her father. Now they were spending time in Montana with her son and his family. Apparently Nina's dad had finally found the secret to fishing that had long escaped him on the Florida coast.

"And how are you, *mija*?" he asked, somehow sounding just as her mom had when she'd used the term of endearment. "How's the ranch? Make any friends yet?"

"I really like it here, actually," she answered honestly. "Molly, the Retreat manager, acts like we've known each other for years. Her husband is nice, too. I also finally met two of the Nash sons." Nina was glad she didn't have to hide the blush that heated her cheeks.

"Oh, really? What are they like?"

"Well, one is the sheriff and the other is a detective, so I feel like you'd really approve of that."

Her dad let out a whooping laugh. Denise must have asked what he was on about.

"My baby girl is living on a ranch with the top dogs in law enforcement," he exclaimed. "Talk about a way to make me worry less."

Nina chuckled and they spent the rest of the conversation talking about his time in Montana. Guilt started to spread through her as the minutes went on. She hadn't told her father about Daniel Covington and the email and she definitely hadn't told him about the fire. She should have told him but Nina knew she wouldn't. Not until the perpetrator was caught. Not until she could ease his mind seconds after she caused it to worry.

They ended their conversation with *I love yous* and *goodnights* before Nina finally crawled into bed.

A breeze blew in from the crack left open in the window above her. The ranch at night was starting to become one of her favorite collections of sounds. Sometimes she could hear the horses, other times she heard owls. Always she heard insects. Their chirps reminded her of home. It usually carried her to sleep.

Tonight?

Thinking of home only made her think of her father and the guilt in her stomach. Which led her to her mother and, as it always went, eventually to the trial. Another detail she'd kept to herself. Nina rolled over. She threw the covers over her head, trying to put distance between memories and the present.

But there she was at the trial. Afraid, sad and wishing more than anything she could become invisible. The press had made that almost impossible. She'd been on the front page of the local newspaper almost every day.

Nina tossed the covers off and sat up, mind racing.

"They're all connected!"

Chapter Nine

A string of surprises had dictated the last week of Caleb's life. He knew those surprises would continue to change his life from normal to a life he hadn't plan. Then, eventually, he'd reach a new normal. It was just how life went.

If it was derailed you could either adapt or crash with it.

That simple.

At least, that's what Caleb was trying to convince himself of as he settled onto the couch that night in the lobby. When that pep talk didn't work, he went to the makeshift break room in the office portion of the house. The bottle of water he chugged was refreshing. The sound of a door in the main area swinging open and footsteps rushing in was not.

Caleb balled his fists and hurried to meet whoever was flying through the next room. He couldn't tell which door they'd come in through, whether it was the front door or the one that led to Nina's apartment. His gun and badge were next to the couch, along with his shirt and pants. If it wasn't Nina then Caleb had one heck of a fight coming.

Luckily it wasn't their arsonist deciding to ambush the Retreat. Nina held up her hands in surrender as they met next to the couch. "Whoa there, cowboy!"

Nina's eyes were wide. She looked him up and down before a red tint came across her face. Caleb might have been only in his boxers but it was Nina who was the distracting one.

Her hair was down and loose, spilling over her shoulders and partially covering her breasts. Caleb was used to seeing her in blouses and jeans—and had no complaints when she wore either—but now she was wearing anything but. Instead, a soft pink silk camisole stole the show, matching a shiny pair of sleep shorts that stopped midthigh. Both gave Caleb a vastly uninhibited view of her smooth, tan skin. It was an arresting image. One he hadn't expected to see. Not even the thin robe that was loosely held around her shoulders could hide the truth.

Nina wasn't just beautiful, she was sexy as hell, too.

Just as her gaze had swept over his body, she took a moment to look down at herself. Her face went from a light red to blazing cherry.

"Oh, my gosh, sorry!" she squeaked out, grabbing the robe and pulling it tight to cover herself. "I—uh—I might have been a little too excited and forgot I was in my pjs."

"We can say you're just trying to match me."

Caleb chuckled and motioned to his bare chest. Nina's eyes once again traveled down his body before snapping back up. Caleb couldn't help but grin. He moved to the couch and grabbed his jeans. Nina hugged the robe around her and looked anywhere but at him.

"So, what's going on?" he asked, trying to land on the reason why she was excited. It felt like it had been a long while since they'd had a reason to be excited. Though, with what Nina had beneath that robe, Caleb could feel the start of some other kind of excitement.

"I found a connection," Nina exclaimed, demeanor changing so swiftly any lustful thoughts about the woman went to the back burner. "Well, at least I think." She hurried closer. Her dark eyes were ablaze with enthusiasm.

"You mean the fires?"

A small dose of adrenaline shot through him as she nodded emphatically.

"Three sites for the fires we visited today sounded familiar, but I couldn't figure out why. That's when I realized I'd seen them…on the front page of the local newspaper."

Caleb felt his brows knit together as he tried to recall any of the stories. While he was tapped into the community much more than most because of the ranch and his job, he'd never been that much of a reader when it came to their newspaper. It was a small press that had been owned and operated by the wealthy, and mostly absent, Collins family. The patriarch, Arlo, owned several more papers across the south. His setting up a press in small-town Overlook had been an interesting business choice that always perplexed Caleb's father. Either way, Caleb hadn't actively read a story from its pages since the top story was Declan Nash being re-elected for sheriff.

"Which three?" he asked, giving up on trying to recall anything of note. Nina held up three fingers.

"The woman who runs the nonprofit animal shelter. There was a spotlight on her because she was throwing a fundraiser."

"Gloria," he supplied. "I remember that fundraiser. She threw that before she opened her no-kill shelter." She nodded and ticked one finger off.

"The Overlook Pass was in one issue I found. The mayor was there for some reason. I can't remember what but I do remember the picture. It took up almost everything above the fold."

Caleb couldn't recall that article. Nina ticked off another finger.

"And most recently, an article ran about a couple trying to bring more nightlife activities for the younger residents to Overlook." She waved him along with her to the office. She went to the recycling trashcan in the corner and rummaged through the papers and empty water bottles until she found what she was looking for. She held the newspaper up, its top story and accompanying picture clear.

"Say hello to Mr. and Mrs. Gentry." Caleb took the paper from her. Nina continued with her spiel. "When I took this job I wanted to learn as much as I could about what goes on around here while *also* looking for opportunities for events and good press. I've only done a cursory look over issues from the last few years and definitely haven't read them all but…" She shrugged.

"I know that's a thin connection, especially for a small town but I thought it might at least be interesting. Three of five places that have experienced fires in the last five years have been showcased as top headline stories in the newspaper. Maybe that's something that can lead somewhere else. Or am I just reaching?"

A spike of adrenaline followed closely on the heels of a memory. Caleb tightened his grip on the paper, staring down at a smiling Kelso and Maria Gentry.

"Four," he answered.

Nina took a step closer. She smelled like flowers. Lavender? Either way it was noteworthy.

"Four?" she repeated. "What? Four places?"

He met her dark gaze. Her eyes really did look like dark honey in the right light.

"The restaurant. Its moving onto the main strip was a big deal. It was an above-the-fold story. I remember Mom reading it."

"So, four out of the five."

"Five out of six, actually," he corrected, anger and excitement starting to mix together. "I didn't have a huge picture or anything, but a case I closed before you got here made it into the paper. Above the fold."

Caleb gave her the paper back and ran a hand over his chin in thought. On one hand, like she said, Overlook was a small town. The weekly newspaper had done stories on almost every aspect of town since it was first published when Caleb was a kid. It could have been a coincidence, plain and simple.

But what if it wasn't?

"It's more than we've had to go on so far, but we definitely need more information," he decided.

Nina went to the computer and turned it on. She must have been too caught up to be self-conscious about her outfit anymore. Her robe opened but she didn't bother to close it. Her smooth, tan skin and curves in all the right places created a ripple effect that reached out to an urge he was having a hard time denying.

Caleb cleared his throat.

There was no time for any of that. If there had been one clear thing about the last week for him, it was that Nina Drake was a woman who stayed behind walls.

And, despite his small attempts to open up to her, Caleb wasn't on the same side.

THE *OVERLOOK* EXPLORER'S website only kept current editions posted and, of those, you had to pay a fee to read more than two stories. Various other internet and social media searches were no help, either. The only story they could track down that coincided with the fires was a blog post written on Gloria's animal shelter blog. It referenced the newspaper article, along with a small, slightly pixelated picture of Gloria and the same two dogs she would later risk her life to save.

When midnight rolled around, Nina and Caleb had nothing more than potentially, well, nothing.

"I guess it's a little too late to go to the *Overlook Explorer* office, huh?" she asked when they'd officially given up on searching. She rolled her shoulders back, trying to free the kink in them. Caleb, in a chair much too low for him, cracked his neck and sighed.

"Usually I'd consider it but I know Lydia, the current editor, takes her sleep seriously. She'd tan my hide *and* probably not help out of spite until the morning anyways. Plus, she'd ask a million questions about why it's so urgent. I don't want any hunch we have on an open investigation to be front page news." He scrubbed a hand down his face. "We'll have to wait until the morning. There's not much we can do right now."

Nina tried to hide her disappointment. Morning seemed like such a long time away. She was too high-strung now to go back to sleep.

Plus, if she was being honest with herself, she enjoyed his company and it was easier to be together with something else to focus on than the things she was still keeping from him about her past.

For a moment Nina worried that that thought somehow showed on her face.

Caleb gave her a quizzical look.

"*Or* we can break the rules and get some answers before then." A wry grin spread across his lips. "That is, if you don't mind slightly breaking and entering. Twice."

A bubble of excitement had already expanded within her. Before Nina had met Caleb she would have asked a lot of questions and, most likely, turned the weird proposition down. Yet, Nina surprised herself by nodding.

"I'm in."

THE OVERLOOK LIBRARY was a stone's throw away from Town Hall. Nina had visited neither. Now she was wearing her dark exercise wear and sneaking through the library's shadows, looking between both buildings with an almost giddy kind of nervous. Her partner in crime was back in his day clothes minus his button-up. His simple black shirt and dark jeans helped him blend in.

Not to mention they looked good as all get-out on him.

Caleb stopped at a side door, the detective's badge on his belt glinting in the flashlight's beam as he swept it up to the lock. He slid the key in and turned. It was like the movement was attached to Nina's stomach. She had to suppress a nervous giggle.

The door opened to a series of beeps. Caleb was inside and running toward the front where the key panel was. Thankfully, he'd already warned her of the alarm. Still, Nina stood just inside of the door in the darkness, a knot of concern. Caleb had the badge, not her.

It took what felt like an impossibly long minute before the beeping cut off. A flashlight beam found its way back to her before the glow showed a purely mischievous face in the tight space.

"I feel like I'm in high school again," Caleb chuckled. He locked the door behind her and then led the way toward the archives.

"You've done this before?"

Even though she couldn't see his face, Nina heard the smile in his voice.

"Since Overlook isn't the most exciting place for a bunch of teenagers, we had to find ways to *make* it exciting. Which includes the one day of the year when the high school seniors try to take the riskiest picture they can to impress their peers."

They turned down a hallway and into the main room. The smell of old and new books filled Nina's senses. She couldn't help but inhale deeply before asking for an explanation.

"Basically, all the seniors trespass on local businesses and buildings and take pictures of themselves once inside," he continued. "The pictures of everyone who didn't get caught are judged at the big end-of-the-year graduation party. There's even a king and queen title if you win." He shrugged. "Sure, it's not the smartest thing to do, and definitely illegal, but it's one of those quirky town traditions. Honestly, I don't think we could stop it if we wanted. Mostly because all the adults *now* definitely did it *then*. It also helps that, so far, no one has gotten hurt or done anything royally stupid." Caleb stopped walking. Nina ran into his back. It surprised a laugh out of her.

"Sorry," he said through his own laughter. "I'm trying to remember which switches turn on the lights in the back room and which turn on the lights in the main room."

Nina gave him some space.

"So you broke in here to take your rebellious senior picture then, I'm guessing?"

"Not only did I sneak myself in here, I decorated this entire place and brought in Missy Calder for a date."

Caleb decided on a switch to flip. Luckily it was the right one. A small hallway next to them led into a room now filled with light. He turned and winked.

"I even hired a violinist from the college the city over to come in. I included her in the picture. Needless to say, you're looking at one of the kings."

Nina smirked.

"And here I thought I was special."

Caleb let out a booming laugh and together they went to the back room. It was a small space meant to do research or study. Two tables sat along one wall with a communal computer between them while most of the room was filled with wooden cabinets, each drawer labeled with a date.

"Since Overlook is as small as it is, if we were going for much older issues we would have to worry about microfilm," Caleb said, sliding right into work mode. "But since we're working within the last five years…"

He scanned the dates on the cabinets closest to the tables until he found the ones he wanted. Carefully he opened the first one and pulled a newspaper out. Nina was gentle, too, as she took it.

A stern-looking Caleb wearing a suit and shaking the hand of the mayor stared up at her.

"The above the fold article of the most recent fire victim. Me." He spelled the information out for her. "Now let's see if we can't find the others, arson or not. Might as well cover all of our bases."

Nina started to follow him but he stopped again. This time she was able to keep from running into him. Still that didn't keep him from turning and giving her another wink.

"And just to set the record straight, I *do* think you're pretty damn special, Miss Drake."

Heat exploded in Nina's cheeks. Luckily she didn't have to worry about hiding the blush. Caleb was already back to work, moving through the cabinets with purpose.

For the first time since she'd met the man Nina felt a sudden rush of worry. Once the arsonist was caught and everything calmed down, would Caleb still be around if he didn't have to be?

And, more importantly, did she want him to be?

Chapter Ten

Caleb spent the next half hour hunting down the issues featuring the Gentrys, Overlook Pass, Gloria and her fundraiser, the restaurant and any mention of Angelica DeMarko, the first fire. After he found each, Nina combed through the articles looking for similarities or anything that could link them.

She was coming up short and said as much.

"I'm not seeing any connection other than they've all been featured as headline news," she said, defeated. A slightly grainy picture of Main Street and the then-new restaurant sat beneath her hand. Caleb's head was bent over a paper in front of one of the cabinets. Nina traced his body with her eyes, appreciating the sight, before her senses came back to her. A sigh dragged her shoulders down, like she was melting into the chair. "I might have been grasping at straws a little too enthusiastically."

"You won't find me upset that we came here. That we tried." Caleb brought his paper to the table and sat down, still looking at the print. Stubble was growing along his jaw. Nina felt the urge to touch it but batted that down. "Part of my job is following leads, no matter how big or small. Plus, there's still some facts that I'm not ready to rule out as pure coincidence just yet." He slid the paper over. The top story featured a picture of a woman and boy facing a house in flames while firefighters worked around them. "Here's the story about Angelica DeMarko's house fire."

He reached over and tapped the edition number and date on the masthead.

"This story obviously ran after the fire," he continued. "But the other stories ran one week before each fire."

Nina felt her eyes widen. To prove his point Caleb fanned out each newspaper until they were side by side. Then he handed her a slightly crumpled piece of paper she hadn't realized he'd been holding. It was a list of the addresses of the fires and their dates.

"The restaurant is a top story," Nina reiterated. Caleb touched the coinciding newspaper and its date. "A week later the fire happens." He moved to the next paper while she read the date on the list in her hand. "Gloria graces the above the fold—"

"She nearly dies saving her dogs a week later."

"And then the Gentrys talk about reviving the Overlook nightlife—"

Caleb slid his finger to the date on the paper and finished her thought.

"And a week later lose half of their house."

"What about Overlook Pass?" she asked. "No one knows for sure when that happened, right?"

"True, but if this pattern *is* a pattern, it more than

could have held. That means it would have burned down a week before you got into town. Almost a month ago. It's plausible that no one would make the trip out there in the time between, especially given the time of year."

Nina looked at the date on the article about Caleb.

"Your story for closing the Keaton case ran a week before the fire at your house," she said, simply. He nodded.

"If you're grasping, then so am I."

Nina chewed on her lips as she looked over each newspaper again. Could there really be something there? Or was it a series of small-town coincidences parading as a hopeful lead?

"They're all written by Delores Dearborn," she said after a moment. "I can't imagine there's that many staff writers for the local paper so that might not mean much," she admitted.

Caleb grinned.

"We won't know until we ask her."

THE NASH FAMILY Ranch buzzed with a restless, quiet energy the next morning. A week's worth of standing guard at their respective posts without any sign of the arsonist being caught was grating on already grated nerves. Molly came in early complaining about a fight she'd had with Clive over "something silly" while Roberto had shown up just long enough to grumble at Nina about the kitchen. She hadn't used his kitchen at the Retreat, and she told him so, but there was no budging his mood.

Then, right before Caleb took off to his brother's house, the eldest one came in hot. Fear gripped Nina, worried there had been another fire, but Declan was venting about lawyers and criminals. After that Caleb and he walked off, surveying the cabins as they spoke. Nina assumed Caleb was telling him about their flimsy, maybe-there lead. Both men stopped near the last cabin, heads bent in concentration.

She couldn't help but feel a bit guilty at how tired Caleb looked.

When they'd gotten back from the library it had been three in the morning. She'd had trouble falling asleep and she'd have bet Caleb had barely scratched the surface himself.

Nina was giving the two privacy by returning to her notebook when the sound of tires made her turn. Dorothy Nash jumped out of her car and greeted Nina with a wide, genuine smile.

"Beautiful day, isn't it?" she sang as she made her way over.

"It sure beats the rain."

Nina could have been working inside but the sunlight had been calling her name. She'd even traded in her blouse and jeans for a breezy dress. An outfit choice that made her a little self-conscious now that she seemed to have lost track of her sandals.

"You got that right, honey!" Smoothing the gray braid hanging over her shoulder, Dorothy stopped next to Nina. "A few years back we had nearly two weeks straight of rain. I'm talking torrential, too. It washed out roads, trees were uprooted and everything was just so dreary. It also put everyone in a mood. Irritable and grumpy. A lot of little fights that were as draining as the dreary skies. When the sun finally came back out for more than a day it was like the spell was broken. Now I can't help but appreciate every single moment it's out."

She sighed and glanced toward her sons. Declan answered his phone. Caleb was looking at them. On reflex, Nina smiled.

"But I'm not here to just talk about the weather," Dorothy continued. The lines at either side of her eyes deepened as her own smile grew. "You know, I was sitting out on my porch, too, this morning, enjoying the view, when I realized we never did throw you a welcome party, now, did we?"

Nina was surprised at that.

"A welcome party?" she repeated. "No, but that's definitely not necessary, especially with everything going on right now."

Dorothy waved her off.

"For every employee who has worked on this ranch, the Nashes have made it a point to throw a little get-together to celebrate." Nina heard "Nashes" but assumed that meant Dorothy was the mastermind. "Nothing too big or fancy. Just some food, dancing and general merriment out at the barn."

"The barn?"

"Molly told me about your idea to turn it into a just-in-case attraction if we ever get swamped by rain. I thought we could decorate it a little for the party while also getting an idea about how we could really tie it in to the Retreat."

Talking to Molly about the barn felt like ages ago to Nina. Since Caleb's house fire happened so soon after their original conversation on the topic, neither woman had revisited it.

"I would love to look at it with you but I'm just not sure a party for me is what anyone needs."

"No one ever *needs* a party, honey," Dorothy laughed. "That doesn't mean we shouldn't have one."

Nina wanted to continue to argue her point—How could they celebrate *her* when one of their own just lost everything?—but Caleb and Declan had made their way over and cut the conversation off.

"Hey, Ma, did you need something?" Caleb asked, his tone softening despite the hardened expression that was reflected on Declan's face. Something had happened. Both men were tense, even more than they had been when Declan first arrived.

"I came by to tell you all about the little party we're throwing out at the barn tonight." Dorothy's eyes narrowed as they swept across her boys. Her eyebrow raised but she kept on. "I was also going to see if Nina would accompany me to town to get some supplies."

"You want to have a party," Declan said, deadpan. "Right now?" He looked like he was going to say more but Caleb touched his shoulder. His smile seemed forced but not unpleasant.

"That sounds like fun, Ma," he said. "Just let us know what time to be there and we will. Right now, though, we have to leave."

Nina felt a pang of disappointment. Caleb had been waiting to call the *Overlook Explorer*'s editor so they could all meet up later that day to talk about the articles and Delores Dearborn. He'd included Nina in that plan just as he had said they both needed to follow the lead from the night before.

But just as quickly as she'd felt disappointment, Nina felt silly.

She wasn't a detective, Caleb was. It was one thing to have her along to look for information when no one else was around. Why would he need or want her when he was actually on the clock?

"Is everything okay?"

Dorothy looked between her sons.

Declan tensed even more.

"Yeah, everything is fine," Caleb answered. "We just need to get rolling." He bent over and laid a kiss on his mother's cheek before pausing in front of Nina. "I'll call you later."

They each left in their own truck, kicking up dirt as they hauled toward the main road. For a moment Nina and Dorothy didn't say anything; they just gazed after the two cowboy lawmen.

The stress both men shouldered was only growing.

It was a feeling that pulled at Nina's gut and pressed worry into her chest. One look at Dorothy and she knew the older woman felt it, too.

"The party sounds like it could be fun," Nina found herself saying. "I'm ready to leave when you are."

Dorothy smiled again. This time it didn't reach her eyes.

DELORES DEARBORN LIVED in one of two apartment complexes within the town limits. It was a nice, clean place with good landscaping and enough parking that Caleb cut his engine no more than a few feet from her front door. Declan had gone to the department to deal with some sheriff-related issue he'd only mumbled about before getting into his truck and leaving the ranch. Caleb was solely focused on Delores at the moment. The idea that she was a link to the fires was probably nothing more than a small-town reporter covering what she was told, bound to write several headline stories over her career.

It could mean nothing.

Caleb was ready to find out.

He knocked, and a young woman with blond curls and a pleasant smile answered the door. Her eyes went to his badge first. They widened when she recognized him. He'd almost forgotten she'd been the one who had interviewed him for the article that ran about the end of the Keaton case.

"Sorry to bother you on a Saturday morning," he said, moving past pleasantries. "Do you mind if I ask you a few questions? It could help with a case I'm working on and I'm kind of on a tight timeline here."

"Not at all." Delores beamed, waving him inside. "Please excuse the mess. I had a late night working on a story." She cleared two empty coffee mugs off the small dining room table and motioned to one of the chairs. "Would you like some coffee? I can make a pot really quickly."

Caleb waved her off.

"No, but thank you. I've already had more than a few cups this morning."

Delores perched on the edge of her seat and slid into a familiar look. Eyes sharp, brows furrowed, jaw hard. She had gone from a slightly flustered, tired woman to a reporter paying rapt attention.

"Alright. So, what can I help you with, Detective?"

"How long have you been writing for the *Overlook Explorer*?"

She thought about it for a moment.

"Almost six years. Though I moved back home to Alabama for a year during that time. I came back eight months or so ago." Caleb made a mental note of that. He kept his detective's pad in the car. If there was one thing he'd learned over his career it was how to keep reporters friendly. In his experience they weren't fans of role reversal, just like he wasn't a fan of being questioned as a detective.

"In that time how many stories do you think you've covered for the paper?"

"Oh, wow," she said around a laugh. "A lot. Um, let's see. The first year or so I actually did more copyediting than writing but since then I've written in almost every edition. Minus the year I was gone. So, once a week for around five years. I'll let you do the math on that one."

Caleb didn't have to do it. No matter what the math added up to, it still showed the same conclusion. She had written a lot of articles because she was one of the few staff writers who worked at the paper. It had to be a coincidence. Still, Caleb wanted to finish asking his questions.

"How many times would you say that your stories have been features on the front page, above the fold?"

Delores had to think about that one too. Her eyes unfocused as she tried to remember.

"Since I'm not a senior staffer and also still do split my time between writing and copyediting, I typically don't cover the stories that land there but I've had maybe about twenty or so while at the *Explorer*. More if you count beneath the fold."

Caleb could see the curiosity in her pushing to the forefront. Soon she'd be the one asking questions so he hurried to his next point.

"I'm going to list out six of your stories that made it above the fold and then ask you a few questions about those, then I'll explain. That sound fair?"

Delores nodded. As far as Caleb could tell, no suspicion had crossed the woman's features. She was no more guarded or worried than he was. It was a breath of fresh air compared to when he had to question obviously guilty parties as a part of his job. There was just something to be said about not worrying that the person you were talking to was trying to figure out if they should fight or flee.

Caleb listed her articles about the fire at Angelica DeMarko's house, the new restaurant opening on Main Street, Gloria's fundraiser, the Overlook Pass, the Gentrys trying to revitalize Overlook's nightlife and the article about his closing the Keaton case. Again, Delores hung on his every word, brows pulled together in thought.

"Okay. I remember all of those," she said after a moment. "Why do you bring them up?"

"Is there anything about those stories that seemed weird? Something that maybe stood out to you or maybe connected them all?"

Delores looked down at her hands folded on the table's top. Caleb gave her time to think it through. If she didn't flag anything then he was going to count this as a dead end. Then he'd go back to the drawing board and hope the arsonist didn't strike again before he found a different trail.

"I'm sorry," Delores finally answered. "I can't think of anything that really jumps out at me other than those were the last six articles I wrote."

"What do you mean? The last six that made it above the fold or in general?"

"In general." She held up her index finger and went into the next room. She came back a minute later with what looked like a planner. "Let me make sure." Caleb saw every day was filled with writing as she flipped through the previous months. She stopped at one in particular and then turned the book so he could see it easier. "The story about Gloria's fundraiser for strays was my last story in the paper before I went to Alabama. Before that, the fire and the restaurant." She flipped forward and stopped again. "And this is when I came back. Marla went on maternity leave so I took over the bulk of copyediting with some website work thrown in. That's why I've only written three articles since I've been back. It just so happened to be three that landed the front page."

Caleb chewed that over for a moment. He wondered if his father would have thought that was enough to be a connection. And *that* caught Caleb by surprise. It had been a long while since he'd tried to puzzle out what his father would have said about a case.

"What's special about these last few stories?" Delores asked. Caleb decided to answer truthfully. Thinking of his father, no matter how briefly, reminded him of one of his father's rules in law enforcement.

Give the truth to get the truth.

So Caleb told her about the five fires that had each happened one week after her stories ran on the front page. When he got to his house fire, he even gave her privileged information that fireworks had been the cause.

"All of this is off the record," he pointed out, after her eyes widened when he was done. "This is still an ongoing investigation. I just wanted to see if there might be a connection or if you had any information I'm missing."

Delores's gaze was unfocused again in thought. Caleb pulled out his card. She apologized and stood with him after taking it.

"It's okay," he assured her. "I knew it was a stretch. Just let me know if you think of anything else that might be helpful."

"I will."

Delores walked him back outside but hung in the doorway as he opened his truck door. For a moment it looked like she didn't know what to say. Then she called out to him.

"The fire at your house... Was anyone hurt? I mean, I assume not because you didn't mention it, but I just wanted to be sure."

Caleb meant to smile, to be polite, but he couldn't stomach it. He shook his head.

"All I lost was everything I owned."

Delores didn't respond. Instead she closed her door with a sinking frown.

Caleb's mood had fallen, too. He pulled out of the parking lot and, for a moment, found himself wishing there was a raven-haired woman sitting there with him. Hours later, sitting frustrated at his desk, that feeling surfaced again.

It left just as quickly as before, though not of his volition.

Jazz's ID scrolled across his phone's screen. As soon as he answered she was talking.

"Caleb, something's happened and it's *not* good."

Chapter Eleven

Caleb met Jazz in the hospital's lobby. Declan arrived separately but timed it just right, walking up to them before she could start to talk. She had her detective's badge around her neck and a scowl across her face. There was blood on her blouse. Caleb already knew it wasn't hers but the sight made him angry. Outside of his siblings, Jazz was his best friend.

"How is he?" Declan asked, phone pressed against his ear but attention fully on the detective.

"Tough to look at." She motioned to the blood on herself. "I barely touched him when I was helping the EMTs get him out of his house and still had this happen." She shook her head. "There's a strong chance he won't survive the night. It's a miracle he's even breathing now. My personal and professional opinion? Whoever did that to him didn't intend for him to live. I think they just got spooked by the girlfriend showing up and bolted before the job was done."

"What do we know? Any idea who did this?" Caleb asked. "Did the girlfriend know?"

"No. She came over after her shift started when she

found him. She heard a car drive off but was too hysterical to look for it. She said that everyone loves him and can't imagine who would do such a thing but, honestly, I think that's just shock talking. We had two people in the last week or so press charges against him." Jazz gave Caleb a wary look. He decided to get out in front of the accusation, whether or not she would make it.

"I called Claire on the way over here and, like every Saturday afternoon, she was at the shop. And Nina has been with Mom and Molly all day. There's no way either could have attacked him."

Jazz held up her hands in surrender.

"All I was saying is that Daniel Covington doesn't have this great track record his girlfriend thinks he does. To be honest, I don't even think she knows about the email he sent Nina."

Caleb pushed down his anger. Even if he didn't like Daniel, what he disliked more was the timing of the attack. The creep who had taken Nina's picture at the stream and then taunted her with it was now clinging to life in the hospital. It didn't feel right.

"I need to talk to his girlfriend," Declan declared. "Where is she?"

"Down there and to the left. They're prepping Daniel for surgery, so Brando is waiting in the hallway with her." Jazz pointed behind them to her husband, who sat with a girl Caleb didn't recognize. "He was already here at the hospital visiting his sister, so that was a stroke of good fortune on our part. He had to use his magic soothing voice to calm her down." She stopped Declan before he could leave. "She's not a fan of the cops, which is another reason why I left Brando with her. Tread lightly with this one. I have a feeling she's close to shutting down on helping us soon."

Declan nodded and was off. Jazz redirected to Caleb. She was frowning.

"Daniel may be annoying but we've never had him pop up on our radar like this before," she said. "The last offense that caught our attention was when he taped that freshman boy to that tree when he was seventeen. Now we have a decent amount of creepiness, harassment and trespassing? And then he gets beaten nearly to death in his own home? Why? What do you think we're looking at here? Another coincidence?"

"I've been throwing that word around a lot lately and I don't like it," Caleb admitted. "Do you know if whoever did this broke into Daniel's place or did Daniel let him in?"

"As best as I could tell he was let in. There were no busted windows or locks. Either the door was unlocked or Daniel let them in. I'm about to go back there now and take a better look. We have two deputies sitting on the place so no one disturbs it." Jazz looked at him with a considerable amount of concern. "Daniel camps out in the woods, takes a picture of Nina, breaks into Claire's office, uses her personal computer to send that picture and then gets caught. He gets arrested for breaking into Claire's and then bailed out. Then he gets attacked and almost killed a few days later. And during all of this, someone burns down Overlook Pass, the Gentrys' house and yours." She took a small step closer and lowered her voice. "We went from a relatively sleepy town to whatever *this* is in the stretch of two weeks? Caleb, what's going on?"

Caleb wished he had a concrete answer.

He didn't.

The night was cool and beautiful.

The town was far enough away that the lights from Main Street didn't reach the ranch. Nina stood in front of the Retreat, staring up and marveling at the stars. They were scattered across the sky like electric sand. Dazzling. Worth more than just a second of her time.

Yet there was somewhere she had to be.

Smoothing down the pale blue dress she'd bought from a boutique that morning, Nina tried to quell the nerves that had taken over since she'd gotten back from the barn. Dorothy, Molly and she had spent the entire day shopping, cleaning and decorating the old red barn a few minutes from where Nina now stood. It was supposed to give them an idea for future ways to entertain Retreat guests but had had a more immediate effect.

Molly's mood had gone from annoyed to cheerful.

The weight pulling down Dorothy's shoulders, despite her winning smile, had turned into a fierce determination.

And Nina? Well, she'd forgotten for a while that her plan to stay beneath the radar and out of trouble had failed. That the only chance she had at a new life was hanging on a Retreat that may or may not ever open. That, even though she was two states away from Florida and the tragedy of her mother's untimely death, smoke and fire had found their way back to her.

Putting together the party had lifted all of their spirits.

Nina inhaled the cool night air before releasing one long, body-dragging exhale. The tension in her shoulders lessened. Her weight shifted the heels of her sandals into the dirt. Somewhere in the distance the melody of insects started up, much closer was the sound of a man clearing his throat.

Her cheeks flushed with heat as she turned. Caleb was wearing what she had come to think of as his trademark grin.

"I didn't mean to interrupt," he said. "But if I didn't, my growling stomach would have."

Nina tried not to look the man up and down—*really* tried—but with the soft glow of the office's porch light behind him, she couldn't help but take him in. All the pieces of his work and day-to-day attire were there. His classic button-up shirt, crisp and fitted, his blue jeans, dark, fit him in all the right places and his boots made up the ensemble she was used to seeing.

Yet it was like they had been repurposed somehow. His shirtsleeves were rolled up and the neck of his shirt was unbuttoned to just beneath his collarbone, showing off some of his bare chest. It was still tucked into his jeans and there was a casual swagger to the way they hung on his hips. Like the artist Michelangelo had painted them on the cowboy.

Or maybe Nina was just full of it.

She'd already noticed, several times in fact, that Caleb always looked good. Smile or not, she couldn't deny he stirred something in her just by being near.

Her eyes slid down and then up his body before

landing on that grin. From there they traveled to those baby blues. There she stayed.

"Did you walk here?" she asked, trying to still the nerves that had just sprung alive in her stomach. Her car was the only one in the parking area that she could see.

Caleb nodded.

"After everything that's happened, I was itching for a nice night." His grin grew. "And just like that, I got one. I thought I'd take advantage of it." He sidled up beside her and held out his elbow. "How do you feel about taking a stroll to a barn that Desmond once told me was haunted by the ghost of the Roaming Mountain Lady?"

Nina surprised herself by hooking her arm through his and laughed.

"The Roaming Mountain Lady?"

"A faceless woman with bangles that clatter up and down her arms, and several skirts and scarves made for suffocating little kids who have the deep misfortune of hearing her moaning in the rafters." Caleb laughed at Nina's questioning look. "Desmond had a flair for the dramatic when we were younger. I think that's why he's so good at his job as a businessman. He's good at helping people see his vision and ideas. He's always been able to spin a story, truth or otherwise, in a pinch. Still, I'm not above admitting that, to this day, the barn gives me the heebie-jeebies. You might have to save my life again if she makes an appearance. I don't think my gun would work on a ghost."

Nina patted his forearm with her free hand.

"I'll do my best, detective. I won't let the mountain lady get you."

They followed the dirt path that led through the Retreat before branching off and cutting through a stretch of nothing but grass. Nina told him about their tentative plans to turn the barn into an indoor–outdoor camping ground in bad weather plus a few other ideas the three women had thrown together as they decorated. The soft sound of music in the distance became louder, pulling them in. Caleb thought their ideas were great but the closer they came to the music and the barn, the more his steps slowed. Nina glanced over and saw his eyes weren't entirely focused on the world in front of him.

"Is everything okay?" she asked timidly. Since he hadn't come right out and told her any news about the arsonist, Nina assumed he'd found nothing but dead ends. She'd decided not to push it, waiting for him to open up instead, something of a pattern when it came to how she interacted with the man. However, this time, her patience ended. Caleb's thoughts were being drowned by something. "Did you get a chance to talk to Delores today?"

"Yeah, I did, but it wasn't as enlightening as we'd hoped." He recapped what he'd learned, ending with a sigh. "I even talked to Arlo, the owner of the paper, on the phone today and poked around a bit. He confirmed what Delores said and even gave her alibis for three of the fires due to work. I wasn't accusing her of anything but Arlo is a good guy and wanted to make sure we knew she was on the up-and-up. I also think he wants her to marry his son, but *that* is just a piece of gossip I heard from Mom."

Nina smiled into the night. The way Caleb talked about his mother, no matter how small the detail, rang clearly with love. It was touching, even if the end of their lead was not.

"So, back to the drawing board, then?"

Caleb slowed to a stop. The back of the barn was visible in the distance. The outdoor lights made the once derelict building glow with joy. Yet Caleb had turned his entire focus on her.

"Nina, there's something I need to tell you." He angled his head down to look into her eyes. She kept her arm around his, breath catching as their innocent contact suddenly felt charged. Caleb wasn't just close, he was holding her.

"Yes?" Even her voice was affected by the change in mood. The one syllable came out as little more than a whisper.

Baby blues swept across her face, two pools of wonder visible in the moonlight. They were just as dazzling as the stars.

Caleb opened his mouth. Then closed it. His lips pulled up into a barely there smile. Nina had a sneaking suspicion he had decided against saying something to her. Something important. When he did speak there was a lightness to it.

"I'd like to have a dance with you tonight, if you don't mind. I'm not going to win any contest with my moves or anything, but I don't have two left feet either. Could be fun?"

The charge she'd sensed heated at the question. Nina felt the rising temperature in her cheeks. It was unexpected.

It was exciting.

"I guess it could be," she answered with a matching smile. "Though you can't get mad if I step on your feet. I haven't danced with anyone since my junior prom." Just like that, a coldness expanded in Nina's stomach.

It was the truth, told in a bout of humor, but no sooner had she said it than another truth replaced it.

Her life in Florida, the one filled with heartache that still managed to touch her years later, was one she didn't want anymore. She'd left it and its memories behind to start over. To live every second on her own terms, not anyone else's.

As Nina swam in the steel-blue waters looking down at her, she knew that to live the life she wanted was to live a life she could control.

However, if there was one thing she was starting to realize, it was that around Caleb, that's exactly what she lacked.

Chapter Twelve

There were no scary ladies, ghost or otherwise, lurking around the barn. Instead, what had once been an eyesore of a structure was now a thing of beauty, filled with people who were trying to forget their stressful week and enjoy one another. Music played through speakers set up in the corners. Wooden tables that had been in the main house's storage had been cleaned and covered in delicious dishes.

Roberto wasn't the only one who had contributed, either. Caleb spotted his mother's homemade apple pie, Clive's homemade-but-legal moonshine and Brando had a good portion of the table's real estate sectioned off for his famous buffalo and cheese dip. Walking in and being hit by the wall of great and familiar smells surprised a feeling of comfort out of Caleb. Most of the employees of the ranch, plus Jazz and her husband, had come at his mother's behest. Like Caleb, they marveled at the world she had set out to create.

"Yeah, it looks nice and smells good but we shouldn't be letting our guard down." Declan came up to Caleb's side with a beer in his hand and a scowl on his face. Caleb chuckled.

"For not having a triplet link with me you sure have a weird way of knowing what I'm thinking," he said. "Sometimes you give even Madi and Des a run for their money."

Declan rolled his eyes.

"I don't need your voodoo triplet telepathy to know what you're thinking, kiddo." He pointed to the table on the other side of the makeshift dance floor. "You keep looking at that table." He pointed up. "The lights and—" He lowered his hand but his eyes skipped to the sitting area that had been staged like a campsite at the front half to the barn. Nina was perched on a tree stump and in the middle of a conversation with Jazz and Molly. "Right at her." Caleb averted his eyes and took a pull from his beer. Declan snorted. "Not hard to put together what you're thinking about."

"Can you blame me?" Caleb asked, lowering his voice so Brando and Jensen, one of the ranch hands who helped with the horses, wouldn't overhear them. "The last two weeks have been insane and yet look at this place. Look at everyone, Declan. They're smiling, dancing and eating some damn good food together. It's a good idea for them *and* us to be here."

Declan didn't look convinced. Caleb sighed.

Out in the field he had been about to tell Nina that Daniel Covington was in the hospital, beaten nearly to death. That the department was digging in to try and figure out who had done it and why. That she had been a suspect, just as he had been, though both of them had been cleared. Caleb had wanted to tell her because in the short time she'd been at the ranch and in Overlook her path had been tied to Daniel's and, maybe the most poignant reason, Caleb wanted to be honest with her.

But then he'd looked into her dark eyes and felt something shift. Standing there in a blue dress with her hair free and flowing, Nina had become someone he wanted to protect. In every way. The whole point of the night was to distance themselves from worry and pain. Did he want to burden her with more?

No, he wanted her happiness.

"If you like her so much, just ask her to dance," Declan said after a moment. There was a smile in his voice. "I'm sure she'd say yes. She ran into a burning building after you, for goodness' sake. Awkwardly swaying to the beat while our mother and friends look on should be a piece of cake for you two."

"I already asked her to dance, thank you very much."

Declan quirked up an eyebrow. "And she turned you down?"

"Actually, no." Caleb hesitated, wondering if he should confide in his brother. Then he caved. "She said yes, but right after that it was like she shut down. Like she'd hit some kind of panic button at the bank. You know, the ones that shoot up those metal walls to protect the teller? Her eyes glazed over and the tension in her body made *me* uncomfortable."

"What did she say? Did you ask her about the change?"

Caleb took another drink of his beer. The bottle was cold in his hand. He shook his head.

"She got quiet after. I mean, we kept up a conversation but it was like we were two strangers battling through small talk. It's not the first time she's done it but I didn't want to push the issue."

"It could be all in your head, you know," Declan pointed out. "Or maybe she's just shy."

Caleb had wondered about both options after they'd come into the barn and gone their separate ways. It was like Nina was avoiding him. She still was. He hadn't spoken to her in well over an hour.

"I thought about that but neither sat right with my gut. I think it's something else. Something I keep accidentally triggering." Caleb paused, glancing at his mother at the food table. She was laughing. "Do you remember how Mom was after what happened *happened*? You know, when we were kids?"

His brother stiffened. "I remember Dad a bit more, to be honest. But I remember she was always smiling to keep our spirits up."

"Even though you could tell she was close to breaking." Caleb hadn't said this to his brother before, not even to the Madi and Des, but now the observation he'd made as a child made him feel it was necessary. "One moment she'd be telling us it would be alright, all smiles and comfort, but then I'd catch her staring off in the distance when she was alone. It was like she'd taken a mask off, the one she wore for her family, and all the fear and worry would be there, in plain sight." He sighed. "That's what happens with Nina but in reverse. Most of the time she's quiet, contemplative, and I swear she does this thing with her eyes that makes me feel like she's a million miles away. But then I'll catch her staring up at the stars or looking at the lights across the rafters, and for a moment she just—" Caleb tried to find the right word but came up short. So he said the first thing that came to mind. "Is."

"She just is," Declan repeated.

Caleb grinned at his brother, letting him know that *he* knew what he was saying sounded crazy.

"I know. I'm starting to sound like Madi when she went through her poetry phase, but I swear Declan, this woman walks like the weight of the world is crushing her with almost every step. And I, well I just want to help." Declan's eyebrow rose again in question. "She *did* save my life, after all," Caleb added. "I just want to repay the favor."

Declan was, and always had been, a straight shooter. He told it like it was, never mind if you were a stranger or family. He just didn't lie and it was as simple as that. It was one of the reasons he'd been elected sheriff in the first place. It was also one of the reasons Caleb respected him as much as he did. While Madi and even Desmond would dance around a hard truth to try and save his feelings, Declan always gave his opinion with a refreshing kind of brashness.

Now he fingered the label on his bottle before meeting Caleb's stare. When he spoke it was with even yet not totally detached emotion.

"Just because someone saves your life doesn't mean you know them. And just because someone saves you doesn't mean they did it because they know you. The best part of this job is when we see ordinary people doing extraordinary things for strangers and that's what we saw with Nina. Not everyone would have gone into that house after you but she did and you two seem to have formed a quiet kind of partnership since. But, Caleb, what do you know about her? About her past? And, honestly, what does she know about yours? Outside of the Retreat business and the fires, have you ever even told her about what happened at Bluerock Park?" Caleb didn't have to answer. His expression must have given away the fact that he hadn't. Declan put his hand on Caleb's shoulder and gave it an affectionate squeeze. "You can't expect someone else to let down their walls and open up if you're holding out, too."

"Someone needs to make the first move." Caleb spelled it out. Declan nodded.

"That's how I see it, at least."

He patted Caleb's shoulder one more time and excused himself. Caleb finished off his beer and surveyed the group and the party around them. His eyes were drawn to the rafters. Strings of lights cobwebbed between them. Out of all of the decorations, Nina seemed to enjoy those the most. Just as he'd seen her staring at the stars in awe in front of the Retreat earlier, he'd caught her glancing up on more than one occasion since they'd arrived.

A small smile would brush across her lips and that invisible weight would seem to disappear. If only for a moment.

Now, across the room, that weight was back. Nina might have been smiling and talking to Jazz and Molly but the way she held herself reminded him of someone standing on the outskirts. Close enough that she looked engaged, far enough that she could disappear at any time.

And Caleb didn't want that.

He put his bottle down, straightened his belt and walked across the room with purpose. Nina watched the walk, her eyes looking more golden than dark in the light, and received him with the same polite smile she'd been wearing since they arrived. Caleb wanted to see the real one so badly he decided exactly what he was going to do.

"Sorry to interrupt but I was wondering if you wanted to join me for that not-winning-any-contests bad dancing I offered earlier?" He held out his hand. For the briefest moment he worried she'd turn him down. Instead, she turned that polite smile to Jazz and Molly and excused herself. Then the warmth of her hand was cradled within his. Caleb couldn't help but reflect the feeling as he pulled her along to the middle of the barn and its makeshift dance floor.

"Now, get ready to have your mind blown by how amazingly fifth grade this is about to get."

Nina laughed and it was just as quiet as her smile.

A new song started just as his boots hit the designated dance area. It moved along a slower tempo than the previous song. Which was a relief. Trying to show Nina she could trust him while trying to keep a bump-and-grind rhythm wouldn't have been ideal.

Caleb slid his hands around Nina's waist and matched the slow pace. She put her hands firmly on his shoulders. There was an undeniable rigidness to them. Her cheeks were tinted red. The thought that he was the reason behind her uneasiness was a new kind of pain in Caleb's chest.

"You know, I have to say, this place looks great," he said to start the conversation. "I was a bit skeptical when Mom told me about fixing it up but, really, I guess it wasn't as bad off as I thought. You did a great job here."

"Thanks," she said, that red tint burning darker. "It was definitely a team effort, though. I've never met someone as driven to throw a party as your mother. I would have given up the moment we ran into this spider in the corner that was as big as my hand." She shuddered. "I voted to leave and never come back but Dorothy rallied on. She is definitely a spirited woman."

Caleb chuckled.

"She definitely is that." They swayed to the beat, holding each other. Caleb traced the woman's face, taking in the freckles along her cheeks as he had the first day he met her. "Mom *is* spirited but that's not the whole reason why she did this. Why she threw this party now, in the middle of everything going on." He took a small breath and then dove in. "You've been in Overlook for about a month?"

She nodded.

"In that time, has anyone told you about what happened to our family? Or, really, what happened to the Nash triplets?"

Nina averted her eyes for a split second. She nodded again.

"I've heard a little about it," she admitted. "I know

you three were abducted but later escaped. And the person behind it was never caught."

A slow wave of anger and resentment washed over him. It always happened when he thought about that day. It probably always would.

"We were eight and being stupid," he said. Even years later he could remember the smells of summer that had clung to them, and the humidity and heat that made them sweat but not enough to deter them from playing outside. He could hear their laughter clear as day, just as he could hear their screams. "Bluerock Park wasn't much to look at back then. No playground equipment or well-kept trails. Just dirt that, if you got lucky, led to a picnic area. Nothing fancy, just some tables and an old rusted grill. But to us? It was anything we wanted it to be." The song grew into a crescendo. They moved along with it. Nina's eyes stayed with his through every movement. "That day we were playing hide-and-seek. I was It so I stayed at the campsite to count while Madi and Desmond hid."

Caleb felt himself draw in. Nina moved her hands around his neck, bringing her closer. He continued. "I'd never heard Madi scream like that before. It was like it came from the trees themselves. It was everywhere. I didn't even know which direction to go in until I saw Desmond running." Caleb hated the next part. Still, he wanted her to know. "The man was waiting for us with a gun already pointed. He told us that we were coming with him and if we didn't that he'd hurt Madi." Nina's eyes widened. She stifled a gasp. A new song poured out of the speakers around the barn. It was slower than the last.

"There was too much distance between us and them, so all Des and I could do was promise we wouldn't do anything. But the man hadn't counted on Madi. See, Dad had been in law enforcement for years, just as his dad had been. He used to tell us that if anyone tried to put us in a car to go somewhere that we were to fight like hell, no matter if they had a gun or weapon, because our chances for survival were more than cut in half once we got into a vehicle. Madi took that lesson to heart. She punched—and I mean *punched*— this fully grown man in the throat. We hadn't even hit our growth spurts yet and there she was, putting force into his windpipe." Nina shook her head in wonder at the young girl's courage. He couldn't help but share it for a moment before getting back to beginning of his nightmare. "It surprised him enough to stagger but not drop his gun. He used it to hit Madi. It knocked her out and enraged Des and me. We rushed him and, for a little bit, the two of us had the upper hand, but then he shot the gun."

"Oh, God," Nina whispered. He tried to give her a reassuring smile. While it had been terrible, they had survived it. A point that he still made to himself when his thoughts turned back to that day and the two that followed.

"I don't know if he meant to miss or was just a poor shot but the bullet grazed my arm." He tilted his head to his left. The scar was still there on his left biceps. It was a reminder. Not that he needed one. "But, man, it bled. Freaked out Des, too. He jumped on the guy's back and just started whaling on him but, you know, we were eight. The man had height and weight on us. He slung Des off on the ground and then—" Nina's eyes widened. Caleb realized his grip had tightened. She didn't complain. He loosened his hold and took a small breath. "He stomped on Desmond's leg and broke it."

"That's horrible," Nina said. "You were children."

"A fact that didn't stop him from threatening to kill Madi if we didn't follow him. He carried her to the car while I pulled Desmond along with me." He omitted the part where Desmond had cried in anguish at his broken leg but still had refused to stop, knowing it endangered their sister. "Then he got us into the car, blindfolded us, and told us to get down so we wouldn't be seen. Normally we wouldn't have listened but, Madi was unconscious and Des couldn't walk by himself. I was the only one who could have gotten out and run but I wasn't going to do that. I wasn't going to leave them."

To this day Caleb felt that absolute resolution that had rung in his chest then. If he'd had a chance for a redo he would have made the same choice over and over again.

"When he finally took the blindfolds off we were in a basement. No furniture but three beds. A bathroom. No windows. That was it. We were there for three days total."

Nina shook her head, disgust clearly written on her face.

"But why?" she asked.

It was a simple yet profound question. One that had haunted him and his family for years.

"I don't know. The only time he spoke to us after we got there was to threaten us with harming the others if we disobeyed him. That only happened when he came down with food, trying to make sure we didn't attempt to escape. After Madi regained consciousness he focused on threatening Desmond. He was in so much pain every single second we were in that godawful place. We didn't want to make his pain any worse... But then we realized the risk was the only way we had to save him from that same pain."

Caleb didn't like any of his story, but this was another part that hurt more than the rest. Nina kept rapt attention on him as he hurried through it.

"We pretended Des had stopped breathing," he continued. "Screamed for the man, cried our eyes out, yelled until our voices broke. For a second I think even I forgot that it was an act. Our captor was absolutely fooled. He dropped his guard when he went to check for a pulse. That's when the three of us attacked."

Nina's eyes widened. It was a look that had been reflected back at him when he told the story to his father and mother after they were rescued. That memory, that feeling of shock and fear and relief at being safe, inspired a truth no one outside the family had been told.

"For all the times I have thought about what happened then, I can't seem to remember how exactly we did it," he said. "We just somehow synced up and became this unstoppable force. Even Desmond with his leg, the three of us overpowered him, managed to buy enough time for us to get to the door, and lock him in. Then we just left. Went into the trees and kept going until a Good Samaritan found us and took us to the department."

"The man was gone when you led law enforcement back?" Nina asked.

He nodded.

"We had been held in an abandoned house just outside of the town limits and deep inside the forest. By the time we could lead them back nothing and no one was there. But that didn't stop everyone from trying to solve the who and why of it all."

He looked around the barn. The music had picked up but he hadn't noticed. They were swaying to their own beat. One that was just the two of them. "My dad was a detective then, and even though we eventually learned to cope with what happened and move on in our own ways, it beat down on Dad. For years after, he continued to work the case. Late nights, early mornings, weekends and holidays. It just…it got under his skin and stuck and there wasn't anything any of us could do about it. He wouldn't listen. Not only had it happened in *his* town, it had happened to *his* kids." Caleb looked over Nina's shoulder. His mother was laughing at something Declan said. Even the sheriff was smiling. It helped loosen the ache that had formed at thoughts of the past. "The reason why my mom felt like she had to throw this party was because she saw firsthand what stress could do to someone. That case, that tragedy, as many people in town call it, sent him to an early grave. He couldn't find any peace and his heart just gave out. So this—" he looked around the barn once more. "This is my mom's way of making sure we see the light in the darkness. See that, even though something bad happened, that something hurt us, doesn't mean that everything is hopeless."

Caleb searched Nina's face. Her focus had never wavered once as he had spoken, empathizing where most people would have in the story, yet now her expression was changing. Into one he couldn't recognize.

After a moment she slid her hand down to his chest. Caleb felt its warmth through the fabric of his shirt.

"Thank you for telling me. I know how hard it can be to carry something like that. Even harder to let it go." She averted her eyes and took a breath so deep her chest nearly touched his. Somewhere during his story and their dance, they'd gotten close. Closer than he'd meant to…or maybe exactly where he wanted to be.

Had she wanted that, too?

Nina exhaled. Her eyes climbed up to his.

"And *I* know this because of the real reason my mother died."

Chapter Thirteen

The mesmerizing glow of the lights twinkling overhead had been doused by an overwhelming darkness. The music cut off so quickly there wasn't even a whimper. The partygoers all quieted for one lost and lonely moment. Fear exploded in Nina's chest. Her breath caught. She clung to Caleb's shirt.

There she had been, for the first time, sharing a moment with someone and having the desire to share back. Nina had seen the pain and sorrow in Caleb's eyes as he recalled what Molly had referred to as the famous Nash triplet abduction. She believed he was genuine in what he said. Nina didn't understand why he was sharing but found herself entranced by the vulnerability behind his blue, blue eyes. It was like she was being pulled deeper into them. Closer to the man until she felt the heat of his body against hers.

He had cast a spell on her with his honesty.

And Nina was going to return the favor.

That's when the power cut off.

"It's probably the breaker," someone called into the darkness. "This place hasn't been used in years."

"I'm closest to the door. I can go check on it." Nina felt the rumble of Caleb's words through her hands against his chest. A small flash of shame went through her at how tightly her fingers had burrowed into his shirt. He pressed his hands over hers. When he spoke again it was directed to the partygoers. "If you have cell phones, pull them out and use the flashlights."

Caleb pulled her hands away but kept one in his own. "Let's go," he said, voice low so she knew he was addressing her.

"Thank you for not leaving me," she whispered, meaning it with all of her being. Shame or no shame, she was terrified of the dark.

They moved slowly as the partygoers started to talk. Small beams of light sprang up on either side of them. Nina wished she had her phone. She'd left it back at the Retreat, trying to embrace the party and its social side with more enthusiasm. She wondered if Caleb had left his phone behind, too. It wasn't like he'd miss a work-related piece of information. The sheriff had been eating pie in the same room last she'd seen him. Not to mention his partner was a few feet away.

Caleb directed them off the makeshift dance floor and past the few chairs that they'd set up earlier that day. Nina's foot caught something. She stumbled. Her hand slipped out of his as she tried to steady herself.

"You okay?"

"Yeah, I just tripped over something." She swung her hand back out until it connected with his. His grip was tighter. She doubted that would help if her clumsy feet decided to take her out again.

They moved around whatever had blocked her way. She could feel his impatience. Not that she blamed him. The darkness was impossibly thick. The only things she could see were the slightly illuminated faces of those who had their phones out. They were far enough away that their light did very little to help guide them.

But they had to be close to the side door now.

"Nina? Where are you?"

The hand around hers tensed. Nina's blood turned to ice in her veins.

Caleb's voice wasn't in front of her, leading. It was behind her.

Which meant the hand she was holding—

"*Caleb!*"

The hand yanked her forward. It caught her off guard. She yelled out again, this time terror garbling her words.

"Nina," Caleb shouted. His voice was closer but felt impossibly far. "Someone bring me a light!"

The barn behind her exploded in noise and movement. The grip on her hand tightened to the point of pain. She dug her heels into the floor and pulled back.

"Let go!"

And just like that, the person did.

The unexpected release sent Nina cartwheeling backward. Before she hit the ground, she bumped into something solid. Two arms encircled her. Nina tried to fight out of fear.

"It's me," Caleb said at her ear. Relief flooded through her but dried up quickly.

"Someone was dragging me!"

Caleb didn't hesitate. He pushed her around and behind him before she could completely right herself.

"I need a light," he yelled again.

"Here," Declan said behind her shoulder.

The light from his cell phone was the answer to a prayer. It moved across her, pausing to make sure she was okay, before going to his brother. But Caleb wasn't there anymore.

"Someone was dragging me," she repeated to the sheriff.

"Stay here." Declan's voice was hard. Nina didn't argue. The beam of light went ahead of him as he swept the area in front of the door. "Jazz, check the rest of the room. No one leaves."

Jazz said she understood. Declan and his light went after his brother.

A few moments later another small light found Nina. It was Brando. She had only talked to the man briefly but now she reached out and took the arm he offered her. Wordlessly, he led her back to the dance floor. The rest of the partygoers had converged there. Some with lights, some without. They waited in silence. Whether it was out of fear or that they were simply trying to listen to any clues that could tell them what was going on outside, Nina didn't know. She watched in muted fear as Jazz took her light and went across the barn.

"It's just us," Jazz confirmed. She came back to the dance floor. Her husband's light showed the detective had a gun in her hand.

Did Caleb have his service weapon?

Nina ran her thumb over her wrist.

Would he need it?

The sound of metal scraping against something outside tore Nina's attention to the wall behind them.

"The breaker box," Clive said from beside her. Molly's eyes were glowing orbs of concern in the dark at her husband's side. He had one arm around her and another placed on Dorothy's, a steadying grip that was easy to see despite the poor lighting. In fact, everyone around her was holding on to each other. Like the survivors of a sunken ship, huddled in a lifeboat lost at sea. Even she was threaded into that group by Brando's arm.

Nina would have stopped to think about how that made her feel, to be included by relative strangers in such a scary situation, but then the power went back on.

The twinkling stars that dotted the spaces between the rafters came to life while the slight thrumming of power vibrated the speakers. Slowly the members of the group disengaged from one another.

Nina was the first among them.

Her gaze caught and stuck on the floor between where they stood and the side door.

"Oh, my God."

Her hand went to her mouth, already trembling.

When Jazz had swept the room for someone hiding in the shadows, she hadn't focused on the floor. Neither had Nina as she walked with Brando to the middle of the room. Why would they?

But now, beneath the lights she'd once thought beautiful, there was no denying someone had been focused on her in the dark.

And way before the lights went out.

"What the hell?" Jazz breathed, following Nina to the first pile.

Caleb hurried through the side door. Nina felt the relief in her chest but couldn't bring herself to express it. Instead she dragged her gaze back to the floor.

Scattered on the weathered wood were printed-out pictures and not just a few. She guessed there were at least fifty between where she stood and the door. Which would have been odd all its own.

Yet the subject of every picture was her.

THE DEPUTIES OF the Wildman County Sheriff's Department spread across the ranch with a vengeance. Nina stood next to one of its best detectives in the barn, trying to detach from the situation as much as she could. The pictures hadn't been touched, at Caleb's insistence. Apparently more people were coming to try and see if they couldn't lift prints from them.

Not that Nina particularly wanted to pick the pictures up. Nearly all of them were visible as they were. Plus the theme was obvious.

"Some of these were taken before we met. Before the stream and the email," she said to Caleb. Since talking to Declan and Jazz he had been circling the area covered by the pictures. Like a creature stalking its prey, even though neither he nor Declan had seen whoever had been in the barn. A point of deep frustration for both men. "I mean, that one over there, the one where I'm laughing and wearing the striped shirt, that's a few days after I came to town. And that one—" she pointed to a slightly out of focus picture taken of her profile as she stood in front of one of the cabins at the Retreat "—I'm pretty sure that was my first day of work. I'm holding my clipboard with my first week's checklist."

"And some of these are after we met," he stated, voice tight. He was right. Nina wasn't the only person in all of the pictures, just the common denominator. Caleb could be seen at her side, just as Dorothy, Molly, Roberto and Clive were in others. However, whether it was because she had spent more time with Caleb than the others in the past week or not, the detective was in the majority of those featuring Nina and someone else. Several were from them around the Retreat. The two closest to her were of them at Overlook Pass. One had been taken at his house the first day she'd met him. When she'd blamed him for the picture and email.

It scared her.

It made her angry.

"I know Daniel Covington said that he just happened to be at the stream when I showed up and decided it would be *funny* to freak out the outsider with the email but this—" she waved her arms out over the closest pile "—this isn't funny."

Caleb let out another frustrated breath. He placed his hands on his hips, showing his badge now prominently positioned on his belt, and faced her.

"This isn't Daniel Covington's handiwork." Nina was about to point out Daniel had already admitted to sending the email but Caleb gave her a look akin to guilt. She held her tongue. "I was going to tell you before the party but decided to wait until later. I didn't think it was connected at the time, but now?" He shook his head and rubbed a hand across his jaw. There was still a smattering of dark stubble across it. "Daniel Covington was attacked in his house late this afternoon. We don't know who did it yet and his girlfriend had no clue, either."

"You think he was too hurt to do this?" She refused to let Daniel off of the hook. He'd already proven how much of a creep he could be.

Caleb shook his head again. "He's in the hospital."

Nina put her hand on her stomach, worry further knotting inside.

"Oh."

"Yeah." Caleb's eyes flitted down. Slowly he took her other hand. Nina's heartbeat leaped at the contact. Caleb, however, looked the opposite of pleased. His thumb ran over her wrist. There was still a red mark where their mystery person had grabbed her and squeezed. "Coming in here to scatter the photos and to do this was…"

"Nightmare inducing?" she offered, partially trying to lighten the mood with a teasing tone while also meaning it.

Caleb ran his thumb over the spot once more. When his eyes were on her again there was an icy chill to them.

"It was incredibly brave *and* stupid. A bad combination," he spelled out. "Whoever did this wants us to know they're still out there."

Nina barely resisted a gulp of fear.

"They want us to know they're—what?—stalking me?"

"Why else go to all of this trouble? And that's what it is. Trouble. This took time to keep up. Again, not to mention, they chanced this big reveal at a party. One the sheriff and other law enforcement officers were attending. They just basically flashed a sign saying, 'hey there,' as though they're taunting us."

Nina couldn't fight that point. The pictures of her were more than damning evidence that whoever was behind this was no longer remaining under the radar.

"If Daniel Covington didn't do this and it's not a prank, then that means that there's someone *else* out there who's following me." Her nerves froze over. She felt her eyes widen as she realized something that had been floating on the edge of her thoughts. "Caleb, what if *I'm* the reason your house was targeted? What if I'm the reason everything you own is gone?"

Caleb's expression hardened. He took his hand out of hers and ran it along the side of her cheek. Nina's body pulsed at his touch but her mind stayed focused on his words.

"You listen to me, Nina Drake, and you listen to me good," he said. "The only person at fault is the person who physically set my house on fire. Whether that's the same person or not, you have my word that we *will* catch everyone who's guilty. And that isn't you. Not in the slightest. Okay?"

Nina breathed in and out slowly to steady herself. She nodded.

"Okay," she murmured.

The detective smiled.

Then it was back to work again.

SAMANTHA NOVAK WAS smiling down at Nina, her braces looking particularly gruesome in the weird light around them.

"You're so stupid," Samantha said, full of glee. "I swear, I don't know how you function."

Nina knew Samantha was fourteen. Just like Nina knew she was also fourteen. They were out on the private beach near their school. Nina was lying on a quilt, the sand around it so white it was blinding. Samantha was hovering over her, still grinning.

"You're going to be late, idiot."

Nina looked around, confused. The ocean was dark and rolled toward them. A horse neighed somewhere in the distance.

"Late for what?"

Nina stood. She tried to brush the sand off herself but it wasn't sand anymore. It was chunkier. Darker.

Samantha's smile turned menacing. It always did when she was bullying Nina.

"Who do you think I am? Your mom? Figure it out, idiot."

Nina blinked and Samantha was gone. The sand was darker, the waves angrier. The quilt was covered in the weird sand. Nina walked away from it, still brushing it from her clothes.

The beach went on forever. Nina was late for something. She just knew it. But what? Where was she supposed to go? It was somewhere close, right? And she was late. So very late.

The urgency pushed her legs faster across the sand and made her heart race. She gripped the keys in her hand. They made the palms of her hands bleed.

She was still late.

Wind whipped her hair around and finally cleared the ash off her clothes. All of the sand around her was swept away with it. Then she was standing on the road.

She knew where she was but that urgency in her still raged on. Being there wasn't enough.

She was *still* late.

"Hey." A man waved to her from the dirt shoulder a few feet away. He was sitting on a patio chair. There was a mug in his hand and a newspaper on his lap. He tipped his cowboy hat to her. "Got it?" he asked.

Nina couldn't see his face but felt such a warmth in her heart that she nodded.

"Got it."

He nodded and opened his paper, sipping on his drink.

Nina wanted to join him, pull up a chair and live in that moment with him forever, but a voice inside of her was yelling a warning.

She was still late.

And something bad had happened.

Metal scraping against metal pierced the air like a gunshot. Halfway down the road Nina noticed a car flipped on its side. Smoke rose from it at an alarming pace. Then Nina saw the man and the boy in front of it in the middle of the road. The boy was staring at her.

Nina dropped her book bag and ran toward the car. Her bare feet tore as they raced across the asphalt. She screamed but nothing came out. She cried but it didn't help.

The boy was running now, too, but not toward the car.

Nina was still trying to scream by the time he was upon her.

"You can't," he yelled, throwing his arms around her.

Nina tried to get past him but he was too tall, too strong.

She heard the *whomp* as something within the car ignited. Flames twisted together with the smoke. They were so close she could feel the heat.

Nina screamed in anguish as the car disappeared. All that was left was smoke and flames.

And the man.

He stood in the middle of the road, smiling.

Nina's body didn't have room for rage yet. She could barely hold on to the pieces of her heart that had just shattered.

She had been too late.

"You can't," the boy repeated.

Ashes from the beach started to fall around them. The last thing Nina saw were three faceless children. One had blood running down his arm.

Then the smoke came and all she could do was try and scream.

Chapter Fourteen

Nina's heart was nearly beating out of her chest. She sat up in bed, struggling to breathe.

No. She'd been too late to save her.

Adrenaline coursed through Nina's veins. She ran a hand across her face. It was wet. The darkness around her only added to the terrified confusion.

Then she heard the insects. A soft melody that wound its way through the woods and fields. The ranch. She was in her apartment at the Retreat.

Nina fell back on the bed, trying to catch her breath, relieved she wasn't back on that road. At that car. Held by arms she couldn't escape, just as her mother hadn't been able to escape.

Nina placed a hand over her sweat-soaked shirt and felt the weight of heart-wrenching memories through it.

She hadn't had one of those dreams in years.

Then again, with the discovery of the pictures of her, and the mystery person trying to drag her out of the barn, she hadn't been this scared in years, either. Try as she might not to, she must have associated that new fear with the old terror.

She let out a long, trembling breath and searched for her phone. It was beneath the pillow next to her. She had no missed calls or texts. Of course, she'd only gone to bed at ten. Now it was just before midnight. The only person she could imagine wanting to get hold of her with new information was downstairs in the lobby.

A distance that made her uncomfortable now.

Caleb.

He'd been the man in the cowboy hat in her dream; even without seeing his face she knew it by how he had affected her. How he made her feel warm. Safe. That's what Caleb made her feel like in the waking world.

Nina blushed despite being alone.

She'd even managed to bring him as a child into her own personal nightmare. The three children had been the triplets, she was sure.

How had one man consumed her thoughts like this in less than two weeks?

Nina threw the covers off and went to the bathroom. She showered off the sweat and exhaustion as much as she could. There was no way she was going back to sleep. Not when that particular nightmare could be waiting in the depths of her unconscious mind.

Being tired was the much preferred option.

Nina slipped into a camisole and jeans and made her way down the stairs. The Retreat side of the house was open between them, as per Caleb's insistence. If she called for him from her apartment, the sound would carry into the main room where he stayed. Even though the only difference was that one door was left open, it made her feel a little bit better.

A ring of light was just inside of that same door, showing that Caleb was still up. For a moment he didn't see her standing in the doorway. She used that moment to take another long look at the man.

He was tired.

He was frustrated.

That showed in how he sat on the couch with shoulders hunched, hovering over a box on the coffee table. It was also reflected in the set of his eyes and brow. A line crinkled above both. His jaw and the dark stubble across it only added to the image of a man who was ready to put their troubles to bed. Even his lips were thinned.

"Knock, knock," Nina said, softly.

Maybe the detective had known she was there. He didn't look at all surprised to see her. Though he did smile.

"Going somewhere?" he asked, gaze running down her outfit.

"It's more of where I'm not going." She walked along the wooden floor, feeling the coolness against her feet. The same feet that had once been bloodied by running across an uneven and pocked road. Caleb raised an eyebrow in question. Nina took the armchair next to the couch. "To be honest, I had a nightmare. An old recurring one I thought was gone." She shook her head but tried to keep her body loose. Not that she thought much got past the detective. "I'm not going back to sleep anytime soon. What's going on here? Any new information?"

He tilted the box so she could see inside. It was the pictures from the barn.

"They were processed but no prints whatsoever. Whoever handled them was probably wearing gloves." Nina had already tried to remember if the hand she was holding had been gloved but couldn't be sure. She had been afraid of the dark and worried. She definitely hadn't been expecting the hand holding hers not to belong to Caleb. "Declan just brought them by. I don't expect him to sleep tonight, either."

"Can I help you look through them? I think feeling useful would help with my mood."

Caleb slid the box to her. She took a handful of the pictures, moved away from the coffee table and sat on the floor. There she started to arrange the pictures in a line on the hardwood. Caleb followed her example so they were seated on the floor next to each other.

"Maybe if we put them in order of time they were taken? At least, from what I remember?" she offered, eyeing the closest one.

"That could help us narrow down who could have taken them."

For the next fifteen minutes or so Nina arranged the pictures in chronological order. At least, as much as possible. There were a few that were just close-ups of her face. Others she simply couldn't remember. Not enough to be helpful, anyway.

When they had done the best they could, they'd moved the chair and the coffee table to make more room. The sheer number of pictures made a shiver run down Nina's spine.

"Eighty-four," Caleb said, voice clipped. "That's how many there are."

"Eighty-four," she repeated. "And here I thought I was doing a good job of staying out of the public eye." She bent over the row closest to them and sighed.

"All of these were taken from hidden vantage points, the best I can tell." He pointed to a few different pictures and cited examples. "The field of tall grass near my house. The trees close to the Retreat and the horse barn. Even a few spots in town have an angle that makes me think the photographer was in between shops. It really makes me wish more kept security cameras outside but, well, we don't have enough crime here for the shop owners to pony up that kind of money. Even though it's been suggested, especially around tourist season."

"They could have been standing in the middle of the sidewalk in front of me, pretending to take a selfie and I wouldn't have known the difference. I still only know a handful of people in Overlook and they all live or work on the ranch." A chilling thought went through Nina. Caleb seemed to pick up on it.

"No one from the ranch is behind this or the fires," he said, confidence clear in his voice. "Trust me. If anything, no one here would be stupid enough to pull this kind of crap with the sheriff and a detective on scene. If anyone on the ranch was going to turn into a criminal, I have full confidence they'd be more subtle."

Nina didn't push the subject. Partly because she believed he was right. What she knew of the people she'd met in the last month didn't quite fit the profile. Then again, people were nothing if not surprising.

"At least whoever the photographer is they managed to get my good side," she noted. "I'm smiling in almost every one."

Caleb's back straightened so quickly Nina's focus shifted.

"There's no almost to it."

"What is it?" she asked.

The detective was scanning the pictures, eyes moving side to side until he focused on the ones near their feet.

"You're smiling in every one of these."

It was Nina's turn to re-scan them.

Caleb was right.

"Eighty-four smiles," he kept on. "That's hard to get naturally on camera that often unless you're waiting for it."

"So, not only are they stalking me but they're stalking my smiles?"

Nina couldn't handle how ridiculous that sounded. They were slipping closer and closer to some kind of Edgar Allen Poe story come to life. One where Nina ended up being trapped inside of a wall at the end. She tamped down another shiver threatening to move across her skin.

"They don't just want to capture you, they want to capture you at your happiest," he added.

It didn't help the creepy factor from rising even higher.

Nina made a sound that fell between a grunt of frustration and a cry of defeat. She fell back onto the couch and buried her head in her hands. The nightmare's fresh wound pulsed new life into the realization of just how little control she had of the situation.

"Do you know why I came here? To Overlook?" Her voice was muffled from her hands across her mouth. She didn't move them.

The cushion beneath her dipped to the side as Caleb's weight pressed against it.

"No, I don't."

The memory of her mother's death tricked her into smelling salt water. The last time she'd sat on the beach and looked out into the ocean without a care in the world.

She should tell Caleb, she thought. Tell him about that day, about her mother's death, about Rylan Bowling. That's what she'd been about to do before the power was cut in the barn. He'd opened up to her. Why couldn't she do it, too?

Because you haven't moved on, she thought sourly. *You just ran away from it and you're ashamed to admit it.*

"Nina?" Caleb's voice had softened. She imagined the blue of his eyes would match the ocean from her dream. Before it turned into a nightmare.

It coaxed her away from her hands.

She was right. His eyes had transformed yet again. Blue waves, lapping over her, making her sink deeper into the sand.

"One day I woke up and realized that if I started over, went somewhere new, I'd have a chance to live a quiet life. And, God, how good that idea sounded. After how loud my old one was. Just the thought of being able to live under the radar. I can't tell you how badly I needed just the thought of the possibility."

She motioned to the pictures on the floor and realized how heartbreaking it was to see them.

"Now I'm back on repeat, just stuck in a different song." She put her head back in her hands, afraid that looking into the detective's eyes any longer would pull out more truth than she wanted to share. "I know how selfish that sounds, especially after what you lost, but I can't help it," she admitted, voice once again muffled. Like she was some kind of child. "It just—it's too much for me. I can't handle it."

The cushion beneath her shifted. Warmth brushed against her hand before Caleb gently pulled it. For a moment she didn't let him move her. But she was starting to see that resisting Caleb wasn't her strong suit. She relented.

"I don't pretend to understand what happened to you, to know what you went through, but I can tell you something I do know." He placed their hands on the couch in the space between them and then brought his other to her chin. Slowly he angled her face up so she couldn't go back to hiding. "It's easier to be alone. There's no real pain there, none that can stick because you can go on ignoring it all day and all night without anyone to call you out on it. After my dad died I pushed everyone away, telling them that I was fine and everything was okay. I had moved on, made sense of what I had once thought was a senseless death, and was just dandy."

A whisper of a smile crossed his lips. There was nothing but sadness there. "But in all of that time, what I really wanted—what I really needed—was someone to ignore me. Because having the burden of pain and no one to share it with isn't doing anyone any good. It's not honoring memories or the fast track to finding closure. It's just a wound that never heals." His smile disappeared. He leaned forward, driving his point home by getting so close she could smell the lingering scent of cologne along his neck.

"And I don't want that for you, Nina." His voice had become deeper. Almost raspy. Something inside of Nina woke to the change. Her breath caught, hanging on to every syllable he uttered next. "You don't have to hide here. Not from me. Got it? You can tell me anything. You can share the pain. I'm here for it. I'm here for you."

Nina closed the space between them, pressing her lips to his in an instant. The kiss was soft and quick. She didn't linger, even if her body wanted nothing but to stay. The flush of desire was burning across her skin, her heartbeat was galloping, her chest was heaving in staggering breaths.

She wanted Caleb.

Did he want her?

"I'm sorry." She sounded breathy but couldn't help it. His words and touch had broken the dam between her desire to be alone and the desire to feel him.

For a moment Nina worried she'd crossed a line. Caleb's face was impassive, his eyes hooded, but then he moved his hand to cradle the side of her face.

And then his lips were covering hers with a hunger that spread through every inch of her body.

Chapter Fifteen

Good heavens, if kissing Nina wasn't exactly what Caleb wanted to continue doing. He could have sworn he tasted a sweetness on her lips. Though he didn't know its origin. Or maybe that was just Nina. Either way, Caleb was drawn in hook, line and sinker.

At least, he was until the less carnal part of his mind spoke up.

For the first time since he'd known the woman she was openly vulnerable. What kind of man was he to take advantage of that?

Did he want to kiss Nina Drake?

Absolutely.

Did he want to do it solely because she was afraid for her life?

Not particularly.

Gently Caleb pulled away. Nina's eyes were hooded, her long lashes dark against her cheeks as she tried to blink away the haze they'd both fallen into. Then it was those dark brown beauties that were searching his expression for an answer to why he'd been one heck of a fool to end what they both had started.

"I—I'm sorry." She stumbled through the words, trying to create some distance between them by scooting back to the arm of the couch.

Caleb sighed. He dragged his hand down his face and hoped he looked like the respectable lawman he was and not a teenager whose excited body wasn't syncing up with his mind.

"No, don't go doing that," he said. "Believe me, there's nothing more I'd rather be doing than exactly what we were just doing, but I don't want you getting the wrong idea about why it is I'm doing it."

Nina's eyebrow rose in question. He couldn't help but note her lips were a bit swollen.

"I want you to know I kissed you because I'm attracted to you and not because of what's happening *to* you," he decided to say. That didn't seem to help with the confusion so he continued. "See, my ex used to accuse me of finding my job more exciting than I found her. That I got too wrapped up in cases. While I don't think that's what I did, at least not to the extent she suggested, I want to make sure you know that I didn't kiss you back because of the excitement of what's been going on. I kissed you back because I wanted to. Truly."

He felt himself soften, giving her a grin he hoped conveyed the trio of feelings he was stomping through—hope, guilt and a little shame, considering his body was still ready to go and ravage hers despite his well-intentioned grandstanding. "Believe you me, I want to pick this back up again but maybe we should hold off until everything has calmed down."

Nina's eyebrow lowered but there was a tightness to how she held her jaw.

"Oh, yeah," she said. "No, you're right. This definitely isn't the time. Not with everything that's going on."

She was off the couch in a second flat. Caleb felt like even more of a dunce. He grabbed after her but she was fast, already weaving her way through the pictures, eyes down and on anything but him.

Most people called him charming, but when it came to Nina Drake he'd had more foot-in-mouth moments than he cared to admit.

"Caleb?"

He was off the couch just as fast as she had been. He wanted to explain himself better, if he could, but Nina didn't seem to want anything he was selling. She'd gone stiff as a board. It wasn't until he was at her side that he realized all of her attention was on the picture at her feet.

"What is it?"

Nina lowered herself slowly. Caleb followed suit. She picked the picture up. Caleb angled himself so he could get a better look. It was one of the few close-up shots. Not much else could be seen other than her profile and smile. The small stretch of background was out of focus and red. Almost all of the close-ups made it hard to figure out location and time.

"I wasn't sure where this picture was taken at first. I mean, where do I even go that has red around me?" Her voice was strained. "But I just thought of something."

She took the picture and walked out of the room to

the back stairs. Caleb followed, his gut keyed up and in tune with the fear that seemed to have crept into Nina's movements. They went up to her apartment without any explanation. There she led them to a door along the wall to the right of her bed. She handed him the picture. Her hand hovered for an uncertain moment over the handle. Then she opened it to reveal a closet.

"How does this look?" she asked.

At first Caleb didn't understand.

Then he saw the red dress hanging on a hook on the inside of the door. Nina stood next to it, staring into the closet. Caleb looked down at the picture. If she had been smiling it would have been an exact match.

"They were in here with me," she said, not bothering to wait for his input. Not that he had any assurances to give. He turned and followed the sightline to the only object in its path big enough to hide someone. The only area that offered any cover was the kitchen. It was small and tucked into the corner of the room as soon as you walked in, but had two rows of cabinets.

Caleb moved around the barstools next to the first row and stood in front of the refrigerator.

"If you were ducked down right there, I wouldn't see you," she confirmed. Her voice fell flat. "And if you were already there when I came in, there's a chance I wouldn't notice you. Though it would be easier to come in while I was in the bathroom."

The feelings their kiss had created were burned away by an anger so intense, Caleb couldn't help the unflattering words streaming from his mouth.

Taking pictures of Nina—stalking her—while she

was out in the open was bad enough. But taking pictures of her while in her apartment?

"Caleb?" Nina's expression had gone blank again. He couldn't rightly blame her. "Could you stay up here tonight?"

He didn't even have to think about it.

"I sure can."

The truth was, even if she hadn't asked, he would have stayed.

CALEB DIDN'T FIT on the love seat in the apartment. When Nina offered him to share the bed with her, an offer that would have surprised her a week ago, he turned it down with a little too much vigor. That smarted but then there were bigger fish to fry than the distance the detective kept putting between them.

Like the fact that someone had been in the apartment with her. She should have seen them. She should have heard them. Yet how often do you worry that people are in your living space, playing a one-sided game of hide-and-seek while taking secret pictures of you?

Not to mention she always locked the door. A point she made to Caleb after he got off the phone with his brother. According to him the only people who had a key to the living portion of the house were Nina and his mother. She kept a spare in a safe at the main house. Nina didn't want to wake Dorothy up so he promised to check on that key in the morning.

Now Nina lay awake in bed, staring at the ceiling and trying not to feel so violated. Up until now the apartment had been her safe space, a place where she'd always felt comfortable. But now it was tainted.

She sighed.

She heard Caleb shift on the too-small furniture. It was mostly dark in the apartment but, given the new information, Nina couldn't bring herself to turn off all the lights. Instead, the bathroom light was on, shielded slightly by the door. It cast enough of a glow that when she angled her head just right she could make out Caleb's legs, hanging over the edge of the love seat.

It had been a good half hour since they'd said anything to each other. At first that had been fine by her but now it made her skin itch. She hadn't been lying when she'd first gone downstairs—she didn't want to fall back asleep. Not after the nightmare. Caleb was supposed to have been her distraction. Yet she'd also wanted his company.

Not because of her needing a distraction. No, it was more than that. In the last week she'd grown accustomed to him being around mornings and nights. Grown used to the charming smiles he offered every time they talked, the way he chuckled when he was reminded of something from growing up in Overlook and the way he had fallen in sync with her despite her always holding back.

He'd never pushed her to talk more than she wanted. In fact, he never pestered her at all. The only thing he'd done was listen to her concerns and theories about the fires and whoever was fascinated with her smile.

She'd never met a man who had treated her with such cool-headed respect.

Suddenly Nina felt like an idiot.

She'd bet stopping their kiss before it grew to more was his way of keeping to his good manners. The very same ones that had endeared him to her in the first place. That's what he'd been trying to say on the couch.

They just didn't make them like Caleb Nash anymore.

And there she had been, keeping the man at arm's length at every turn.

Sure, she had been about to open up to him in the barn, but after the commotion she'd been slightly relieved for the interruption.

What was she so afraid of?

Was sharing such a key moment in her life what really scared her or was it being vulnerable?

Nina sat up in bed.

"Caleb?" she whispered, hoping she wouldn't wake the man if he had fallen asleep. Judging by how quickly he answered, she hadn't.

"Yeah?"

Nina took a deep breath. The darkness was oddly emboldening.

"I was fourteen when my mom died," she started without a segue. She just needed to finally get it out. "We were supposed to go shopping in town but I'd followed some friends to the beach after school. This awful girl named Samantha Novak had shown up with her cronies and we all started doing that high school thing where you just kind of insult each other before the winner eventually leaves. I realized too late that I'd lost track of time and had to run home. There was this street that was a shortcut between our house and the private beach. No one really used it. There were potholes everywhere, it was uneven, and it had trees and construction on either side of it. Not something most people took when they could stay on the main streets and have an ocean view."

The image of the street from her dream rose to the front of her mind as well as Caleb sitting off to the side of it with his coffee and paper. "Mom knew I was at the beach and, since she'd shown me the shortcut when I was little, knew I'd take it home. Dad had said she'd told him on the phone that she'd had a bad day at work and was impatient to get out and stretch her legs." Nina paused, smiling slightly at that detail. Only her mother counted walking around the outlet mall and eating snow cones or giant pretzels as "stretching her legs."

That smile didn't last, and neither did the affection there. Now she was diving into the worst day of her life.

"Her car was already on its side when I got there. Another car had hit her and pushed her off the road. It took me longer than it should have to realize she wasn't the one standing in the middle of the road. It was a man. He was just looking at the car. That's when I saw the smoke and flames. Then I realized she was still inside."

Pain lit up Nina's chest. She pushed past it. "I ran as fast as I could, but a boy met me before I could get there. He was the son of the other driver. He'd run to a nearby house to call the cops, and when he saw me running toward the fire had decided it was too dangerous.

He held me there as the car became engulfed in flames. Held me there while I screamed and cried. Stayed until my dad showed up...which is why he didn't see that his father watched my mom's car burn with a smile on his face. I'll never forget it for as long as I live. He just smiled."

Nina took another steadying breath. This part of the story brought in a deep, dark anger. She became lost in it. Caleb's voice sounded far off, like an echo in a dream.

"I'm so sorry, Nina. I can't imagine going through that."

Nina snapped back to her senses. She still wasn't through with her story but she'd already come this far in sharing it with him. She might as well end it.

"I'd like to say all the horrible ended with that day, and every day after was just us trying to grieve and move on, but then the trial happened. Apparently my mom's bad day had to do with a man she worked with named Rylan Bowling. She'd had to fire him that afternoon for harassing another female employee. He hadn't taken it well. Threatened her. And, well, you can guess how it played out from there. He saw her on the road, followed her, rammed into her when no one was around and didn't help her when he could have. You would think this was an open-and-shut case, but he got some fancy lawyer from up north. Said it was an accident. It made everyone nervous that he'd get away with it. So I offered to be a witness."

Another detail Nina wouldn't forget was how her palms got sweaty, her stomach turned and how truly terrified she was during the trial. But she'd wanted nothing more than to have that man pay for what he'd done. "I told them about the smile and then his son, Jeremy, told them he couldn't confirm or deny it since he'd been too focused on keeping me safe. Along with everything else, the jury was convinced. Rylan Bowling went to prison, and Jeremy and I made all of the papers. The daughter who was saved by the son sends his father to prison for killing her mother. The media really loved the poetry of it. They even ran anniversary stories once or twice." She snorted. It held no amusement. "Jeremy left town to live with some relative and I stayed. After everything that had happened, I guess I started hating the spotlight. Then that kind of turned into shying away from any normal attention, too. It became who I was. Then, one day, I realized that, even though the spotlight had faded, the memories of it never would."

"So you came here, hoping to stay beneath the radar. And instead got caught up in whatever the hell it is that's going on."

Nina nodded in the dark.

"I used to not believe in bad luck, but I tell you what, I'm starting to lean toward believing it," she half-joked. "Either way, I wanted you to know."

Caleb was quiet a moment. Then his voice was a whisper in the dark.

"Thank you," he said simply.

It was enough to make a difference. The weight of her memories somehow felt lighter now that she'd shared them. Maybe there *was* something to talking about things.

Nina settled back into the sheets.

Caleb continued to move around, undeniably uncomfortable on the small furniture.

"And Caleb?" she called.

"Yeah?"

"Let me sleep on that ridiculously small couch or come to bed. Those are your options."

The detective played it smart.

He came to bed.

Chapter Sixteen

It started out innocently enough.

Caleb stayed, fully dressed, above the covers; Nina didn't think it nice to force him beneath them. She kept as much distance between them as she could in the full-sized bed. They said goodnight and then quieted.

But then Caleb got a call and that put them on a downward slope that only really had one outcome.

"Sorry," Caleb apologized for the third time before he reached for and answered his phone.

Nina didn't mind. A phone call this late had to be important. She just hoped it was good news and not worse news.

"Caleb Nash here," he answered, voice flipping straight to business.

Nina wanted to inch closer to hear the person on the other end of line but thought better of it. Caleb had been nothing but forthcoming about everything so far. If he thought she should know what was going on then he'd tell her.

Though that didn't stop her from straining to listen.

Whoever was on the other end must have been soft-spoken. She couldn't hear anything.

"Okay, yeah," Caleb rattled off at intervals throughout his conversation before ending with, "Thanks. I'll see you tomorrow."

The bed shifted under his weight as he put his phone back on the nightstand. Nina tried not to seem overeager. And immediately failed. "Everything okay?"

The bathroom light outlined the detective. He had moved onto his side and was facing her now. It made Nina's body react more than she cared to admit.

"That was a friend of mine at the hospital. I asked her to let me know of any significant changes with Daniel Covington."

Nina wasn't a fan of Daniel's, by any means, but for a moment she worried he'd passed away. Sure, being a creep wasn't the greatest, but he definitely hadn't deserved the beating Caleb described. "Apparently the kid made a turn for the better. He might even be able to talk to us tomorrow."

She wondered if she was a part of the "us" but decided not to ask.

"Hopefully he can tell us what happened and who almost killed him," Caleb added.

Nina heard him sigh. She couldn't help but reach out. She fanned her fingers across his chest, hoping to offer some kind of comfort.

"You'll figure it all out and everyone will get what's coming to them," she said, confident. "If there's one thing I've learned in my limited time with you all it's—you don't give up."

She couldn't see his smile but imagined it there as she felt his touch when he placed his hand over hers. Nina worried that she'd overstepped until he ran his thumb across her knuckles. It was a slow, tantalizing motion.

That's when Nina knew they were doomed to fall prey to the inevitable. Their kiss earlier had pushed over the first domino in a series of pieces leading to a conclusion they could no longer avoid. At least, Nina didn't want to. Not after being this close to the man she should have realized sooner made her feel absolutely safe. A feeling she hadn't had in a long, long time.

"Caleb—" she started, unsure of what she was going to say. Thankfully, she didn't have to figure it out. His touch transferred from her hand to her wrist. From there his fingers skimmed along her bare skin up her arm. Nina barely contained a shiver of pleasure at the contact. When his hand trailed over to the side of her neck, Nina knew whatever resistance she might have had in reserve was gone.

The space between them disappeared.

Nina angled her lips up, easier to be found in the dark.

Not that Caleb had any problems.

His lips were warm and diligent. They pressed against hers with insistence. Nina had to dig her fingers into the fabric of his shirt just to steady herself from the onslaught of excitement running rampant through her. He deepened the kiss at her display. Nina moaned against him, unable to hide how much she wanted this.

Caleb seemed to agree.

He let go of the side of her neck and grabbed her hip through the blanket. On reflex Nina tried to push closer. Frustration broke through her haze long enough to break their embrace. Caleb was on the same page. She didn't have to complain about the layers separating them. He was already sliding beneath the same sheets.

They collided again. This time there was more urgency there. One of his hands wound into her hair while the other grabbed her hip again, pulling her flush with him. Nina moved against him, feeling his excitement, before she decided she needed to be closer. She slid her hands up his shirt, marveling at the firmness beneath, until he was forced to pause so he could rid them of the annoyance. Nina took that time to mimic the action. She threw her own shirt away from their island of sheets and darkness.

A gasp escaped her lips as Caleb appreciated her now-bare chest. He kissed down the slope of her breast before directing his tongue to her nipple. It beaded instantly. Nina moaned again.

Another instantaneous reaction.

Caleb crashed back into her lips, his hands hungry against her body. Nina reached out, just as ready. She pulled at his jeans and before she knew it they were gone in the darkness, too.

Then Caleb was above her, straddling her.

He was gentle as he lowered himself to her lips. His kiss was a whisper.

"You're one hell of a woman, Nina Drake."

Nina couldn't help but grin.

She had spent so long trying to live a quiet life that she'd forgotten that not all excitement was worth missing.

"You're not so bad yourself, detective."

CALEB WOKE WITH the sun on his back and a beautiful woman in his arms. Not what he had planned but he definitely wasn't complaining. Nina was fast asleep, her bare back against his chest and her hair splayed out on the pillow they shared. When Caleb had first gotten into her bed he had noted its small size. Now he appreciated how it worked perfectly when he held her.

Nina stirred against him. Caleb enjoyed the sensation. He wouldn't have minded exploring it further when she woke up, but along with the sunlight, the duties he needed to perform for his job started to filter through. As carefully as he could, he pulled his arm from beneath the pillows and lifted the one around Nina's waist. The raven-haired beauty shifted onto her stomach but didn't wake. Caleb checked his phone.

He'd always been an early riser—one of the perks of being raised on a ranch—and was glad to see it hadn't failed him despite his active night. It was six-thirty. Plenty of time to get ready, eat and head out to the hospital. He slipped out of bed, felt the chill of the air conditioner against his naked body and strode off to the bathroom. When he came out, dressed, Nina was awake and sitting up in bed.

She smiled a little uncertainly. The sheets were up around her chest. There was a blush on her cheeks.

"Good mornin'," he drawled in his most Southern accent. Over the last week he'd noticed how Nina would smile when his Southern twang slipped out.

"Good morning," she repeated, her smile growing. She motioned to the bed. "Sorry if I was a bed hog."

Caleb went over and kissed her full on the lips.

"I have no complaints here," he assured her.

Nina nodded.

"Good," she said. Her expression went from open and sweet to determined. She eyed his phone. "So, what's going on? Are you going to go see Daniel Covington?"

"I am, but not until after breakfast." He patted his stomach dramatically. "I seem to have worked up an appetite after last night."

Instead of falling back into her quiet, slightly detached ways, Nina surprised him. She laughed and sent him a wink.

"Now that's a workout I can get used to."

A deep-chested chuckle escaped Caleb before he gave her one more kiss and then got to work. He excused himself and called Declan to update him about Daniel Covington before calling Jazz. She sounded much less enthused.

"I hope he can tell us who the heck attacked him because I haven't been able to track down anyone who can," she said, irritated.

"I want to know who else had an interest in Nina," he said. They had already talked about the possibility of Daniel knowing the person who had cut the power at the barn. The picture he had taken of Nina and sent in the email was framed differently than the ones left across the barn floors, but that was too much of a co-incidence to pass off as unrelated. "I bet my bottom dollar he knows who that sonofabitch is."

Jazz agreed with an added huff.

"We need a win somewhere," he said. "Between this and the fires I think some people around here are losing morale. Roberto was even talking about heading to his parents' place until all of this chaos was controlled. His words, not mine."

Caleb didn't blame Roberto for what he'd said, though it grated that someone from the ranch would consider leaving it because they felt unsafe.

They ended the call by agreeing to meet up after he went to check on Daniel. Then Caleb turned his attention to Nina. She had dressed in an open flannel shirt with a black skinny-strapped thing beneath it and pair of jeans that acutely reminded him of how long and smooth her legs were, despite her petite frame. She even had on a pair of boots that went over her jeans at the ankle. Her freshly washed hair was pulled back in a wet braid.

"If you don't look like a bona fide cowgirl," he said, admiring her. "All you need is the hat and you're cooking with gas."

She laughed.

"Never thought I'd be called that, but I'm not going to lie, I'm not against it." She sidled up to him and that concern came back. Caleb had never met a woman who went from lighthearted to down-to-business so quickly. He wondered if his changes between the two were just as abrupt. "I don't think I should go with you to the hospital," she said, sure in her words. "Not that you asked me to go or anything, it's just that I wanted you to know that I prefer not to."

Caleb had been on the fence about inviting her along. He was glad she'd brought it up first.

"I don't want to see Daniel in bad shape any more than I want to see him in good shape," she continued. "I think my emotions might get the better of me. I might say something I'd regret later."

Caleb nodded. He'd been there before as a rookie. There were some instances where it had been a struggle for him to keep his cool talking to men and women who had done things he definitely hadn't approved of.

"Do you mind hanging out at the main house while I'm gone? Mom offered to make breakfast for us last night before we left the barn." He gave her a soft smile. "She's worried about us worrying. Plus, I'd also worry less with you not being alone."

There was a softness to his words. A touching concern that Nina appreciated.

"That sounds wonderful."

They made their way five minutes up the road to the main house. Declan's truck was in the driveway. When they went inside he was asleep on the couch. Caleb's mom descended the stairs with her index finger pressed against her lips. She waved them to follow her out to the back porch. Caleb should have been surprised that there were covered plates of eggs, bacon, biscuits and gravy but he wasn't.

When Dorothy Nash was trying to keep her own

stress levels low, she cooked. It was therapeutic for her. It threatened the rest of their waistlines.

"Your brother was up until dawn," she said once the back door was closed behind them. She motioned to the benches on either side of the table. "That man will avoid sleep at any and all costs if I don't holler at him about it."

Nina took the spot next to his mother and the three of them immediately went to eating. To his mother's credit she didn't talk about what had happened at the barn and instead kept talking about the Retreat. It seemed to be exactly what Nina needed. Work talk energized her, and before long the two of them had commandeered a notebook where they wrote out their ideas for future events for the ranch. The decision to open on schedule or postpone wouldn't be made until the next day. Neither woman let that worry them. Caleb believed that to be in partial thanks to his mother. She let Nina know right then and there that, even if they delayed opening, Nina's job was still secure. That, plus his mother refused to let someone take away her dream of the Retreat without fighting for it. So, until she said otherwise, they would continue to plan for every eventuality they could think of, which included events from the grand opening party to months away. One in particular caught Caleb's fancy.

"A good old-fashioned dance out under the stars," he repeated. "We could invite the town to that. You know Jazz's husband, Brando, is in that band. I heard them at the bar once and they were pretty great. I'm sure they'd loved to play it." He smiled at Nina.

"Though I suppose I might need to figure out that dancing thing beforehand."

Nina returned his grin.

"I think you managed just fine before."

His mother looked between them. Then she was beaming. Caleb was sure the next time they were in private their main topic at hand would be the dark-eyed beauty from Florida.

Caleb had to say goodbye once his food was finished. Both women adopted looks of concern but neither voiced them, which he appreciated. He already felt guilty about leaving them, but he had to do his job. Despite his mother's objections he woke Declan up on his way out and made sure he'd keep an eye on both women. Declan promised and then Caleb was in his truck, staring at the house in the rearview.

He couldn't help but wish he'd grabbed a kiss for the road.

THE HOSPITAL WAS QUIET. Caleb met his friend Katie in the hallway outside of Daniel Covington's room. She got right down to business.

"That kid is a freaking miracle." She greeted him, pulling a peppermint from her scrubs pocket. She worked third shift and would be leaving soon. Caleb had grown up around Katie due to her close friendship with Madi. She had occasionally helped the sheriff's department, namely him and Declan, with her expertise and connections to the hospital and her colleagues' insights. "He shouldn't even be awake, let alone able to talk." She shrugged with a sigh. "But, you know, youth and all of that. If that had been me I think my body would have already called for the check."

"So I can talk to him now?"

She nodded.

"I'll warn you, though. He's still medicated. He might be able to form words but I don't know how much of those words you should trust." Caleb thanked her and started for the door. She held out her hand to stop him. "I have to ask, does he need a lawyer here? I mean, I love you Nashes, but I've got two kids at home who need their mama to not get sued if this all goes sideways."

Caleb smirked. Katie had always been clever. Even when they were kids she'd been fierce.

"He was the victim this time. I'm just here to see if I can figure out who did that to him and see if he has any connections to another case I'm currently pursuing."

Katie smiled and waved him past.

Daniel's room was small but private. The rhythmic beeping of a heart monitor indicated the young man lying on the bed, propped up and looking like hell, wasn't out of the woods yet. Caleb was glad Nina wasn't here to see him. With or without a connection with the kid, it was hard to see at how bad off he looked.

"Hey, Daniel," Caleb greeted the boy, catching his eye. He moved slowly to the other side of the bed and pulled up one of the two chairs next to the window. "Do you remember me?"

It took a few seconds but then there was a small nod.

"Good. Well, I'm here to ask you a few questions,"

Caleb continued, using a soothing voice he adopted for sensitive situations. "I was wondering if you remember who did this to you. Who attacked you yesterday morning?"

Daniel's eyes widened but no sound came out. Instead, he looked around the room, moving his head slowly to gauge it in its entirety.

"Can you talk, Daniel? Do you understand me?"

He moved his head back. His gaze slid slowly up to Caleb's. He opened his mouth a few times before any words formed.

"You alone?"

Caleb leaned forward.

"Am I alone? Yes, I am. I wanted to talk to you as soon as possible so I could figure out who did this to you."

Daniel seemed okay with this answer. He licked his lips and blinked slowly before speaking again.

"—paid me but—but I didn't know…"

Caleb tried to keep his mounting frustration tamped down. Katie was right. It was a miracle Daniel had even survived, let alone could talk.

"Someone paid you," he tried instead. "Who paid you? And to do what? Get beaten up?"

Daniel inhaled loudly and let it out with a wince. Caleb wasn't the only one frustrated by the situation.

"He said—it—was for camping." Daniel paused, confusion changing his expression before he seemingly regained his train of thought. His brows pulled in together, disapproval cascading over his bruised and scabbed face. "…didn't believe him. Then she called—and—" Daniel's hand made the smallest of waves.

"Then you were attacked," Caleb guessed.

A small, barely there nod confirmed it.

Caleb took a steadying breath. He didn't want to push the boy but he wanted answers. Needed them.

"Daniel, who attacked you?" Daniel's eyelids were drooping. "Daniel? Who attacked you?"

Caleb believed Daniel was really trying to be cooperative but the miracle man was already low on steam and losing it fast. Only one answer came out of his lips before he slipped back to sleep, pulled under by exhaustion and pain medication, but Caleb still heard it clear as day.

"Kerosene."

Chapter Seventeen

The sky looked like it had been flipped upside down. One moment it was sunny and blue, the next it was as dark and menacing as the bruises across Daniel's body. The darkness cast ominous shadows inside of the sheriff's department. They reached out and made the whiteboard set up between his and Jazz's desks even more daunting.

"Daniel, the fires and the incident at the barn," Jazz said, reading out the three headlines along the three timelines they'd reconstructed. She tapped the spot beneath Daniel's line. "He said he was paid to do something and all we know that he's done is take the picture of Nina at the stream and then send it from Claire's. He also dramatically said 'kerosene.' And then you were kicked out before he could corroborate anything at all."

Caleb nodded.

"It wouldn't have mattered if I'd stayed. That boy is going to be out for a while. Katie was right. It was a miracle he was able to say what he did. She said her husband would give one of us a call if anything changed. He's working day shift on the same floor as a nurse."

Jazz shrugged, attention back on the whiteboard. She moved to perch next to him on the edge of the desk facing it. "So, what's your gut telling you, cowboy? Because mine is saying we're missing something."

Caleb was quiet a moment. He'd already gone over what they knew three times since they'd started. It made him angry every time he spoke of the parts that included Nina, knowing how scared and violated they had made her feel. He rubbed his chin and started back at the beginning.

"Daniel took the picture and sent the email. No denying that. But there's no way he was at the barn. Honestly, my gut is saying he had nothing to do with it. The pictures at the barn were all similar. Nina's face was always visible and she was smiling. The one Daniel took was of her back. He also left a message about everyone thinking she was a good girl." Caleb's jaw clenched in fresh anger. He pushed past it. "There was no message at the barn."

"But they tried to grab her at the barn," Jazz pointed out.

"Daniel could have easily grabbed her from Connor's Trail. Either before I showed up or after she left the stream. If the goal was to get Nina, then he had the perfect opportunity."

"*And* Daniel wasn't at the barn," she said.

"No. He wasn't. But if he was working with the person who was, they're not on the same page about what they want."

"Which seems to be Nina."

"Which seems to be Nina," he repeated.

"Okay, so Daniel is paid by—who? Nina's stalker? Statistically stalkers are loners. Not to mention, what's the point of using Daniel at all to send the email? Especially if they're going to do something as daring as what happened at the barn while Daniel had one heck of an alibi."

"It makes no sense," he agreed.

"And we're not even touching on the fires yet."

A thought occurred to Caleb, stirred by a memory. Then it was like the flood gates had opened.

"Daniel was a distraction." As soon as he heard it out loud, Caleb believed it to be true. He went to the whiteboard and touched Daniel's name. "He's paid to take Nina's picture and send her the email. We arrest him and suddenly he has a lawyer who gets him out." He touched the note about Daniel being attacked. "But then he has a change of heart because he's told something he didn't know and investigates. He finds—" Caleb touched the one word that he'd have preferred to be the name of whoever was behind the barn incident. "Kerosene. He said it was for camping."

Adrenaline shot through Caleb at the rush of seeing something he'd missed. He jabbed the spots on the whiteboard beneath the Gentry's house fire and the one at Overlook Pass.

"Kerosene was used as an accelerant at both. Did you hear what the fire chief said about kerosene?"

Jazz nodded, standing. The look of excitement he recognized from leads panning out crossed her expression.

"Yeah, that it's not a popular tool for arson because of the smell and how careful you have to be to use it. There are much easier and less deadly ways to start a fire."

"But what if there's a reason you use kerosene?"

He picked up the dry erase marker and wrote down *Angelica DeMarko* at the beginning of the timeline for the fires.

"This is the only fire to not be related somehow to a front-page story in the paper that ran a week before it took place. This fire spread so quickly because it hit camping supplies, namely kerosene."

He tossed the marker to Jazz, who caught it, and then went to his computer. He started a search, emboldened by a potential connection.

"So, what? You're thinking Angelica is our arsonist? Kerosene was only at two of the four other fires," Jazz pointed out. "Not to mention yours was started by fireworks. Once arsonists find their grooves, pathologically they usually have to stick to that method, like a serial killer might. Breaking that pattern would be nearly impossible for them. And how does that tie in with Daniel?"

Caleb didn't respond. Not yet. He was working through a hunch, one that he knew was a long shot. A hefty, long-wing-spanned stretch.

Then he found what he was looking for and felt another wave of excitement.

"I don't think Angelica had anything to do with the fires. She hasn't been back since she left town for a better job out of state." Caleb looked at Jazz. "But her son, Jay, was cited for drunk and disorderly in town a month before the Gentry's house fire."

"That's a stretch, Caleb," she warned.

"Oh, I know," he said, breezing past it. "But what if, after Jay watched his house burn, he realized he liked it? It triggered something in him."

Jazz continued to look skeptical. She opened her mouth to argue but then closed it fast. Her eyes widened.

"Caleb, he was the grill cook."

"What?"

This time she went to her computer and did a search. Caleb hurried around his desk to look at her screen. She pulled up a picture of the newspaper article about the fire at the restaurant that he'd taken at the library. She pointed to one of the last paragraphs. It was a quote.

From Jay DeMarko.

"He said he looked away for a few seconds before the fire started," she paraphrased. "He was the grill cook."

"This might be a stretch but it's more than we've had in a while," Caleb said, grabbing the keys off his desk before going back to his computer. He wrote down the address on his screen. "I say it's time we go have a talk with Jay DeMarko."

"You think he's trying to make us think he's a stalker when really he's our arsonist? But how does Daniel fit into this?"

"I don't know. This could be nothing, just me trying to find a win," Caleb admitted. "Or we could have just found our missing piece."

THE RAIN HELD off as Caleb and Jazz drove to Jay's apartment. Instead the air was filled with that same electric charge that he'd felt the day his house had burned down. It was foreboding. Caleb hoped it wasn't a sign of bad things to come.

He parked his truck outside a set of stairs that led to the second floor unit that was listed on Jay's citation. His brows knitted together.

"Delores Dearborn lives right there," he said, pointing to the apartment on the ground floor.

"Eerie coincidence?" Jazz asked, checking her service weapon discretely below the dashboard. Caleb followed suit.

"I'll let you know."

They had both donned their blazers, a tactic they adopted when they had to deal with potential suspects. It hid their guns and badges until they were ready for either to be seen. Hiding the badge especially kept perps from running before they ever got a chance to talk to them. Caleb straightened his to make sure the badge on his hip wasn't peeking out and went up the stairs. He knocked on the door. The force pushed it open.

Caleb and Jazz shared a silent look. Both pulled out their guns and held them low.

"Hello?" Caleb called, cautiously. From his vantage point the living room was empty.

No one responded.

"This is the Wildman County Sheriff's Department," he tried again. "We're here to talk to Jay DeMarko."

Again, no one replied.

Caleb and Jazz nodded to each other before they entered the apartment.

It was the same layout as Delores's downstairs unit. Caleb led the way as they cleared the living room, kitchen and bathroom. There were two doors left. The first was open. It was a bedroom. Sparse, no sentimental items or decorations. Caleb opened the closet. Also sparse. Only a few shirts were on hangers. There was a closed suitcase on the floor. Caleb decided to come back to that after they checked that the last room was clear.

This time Jazz led the way. He threw open the next door as she rushed in, gun drawn. She was met with no resistance but Caleb heard her gasp clear as day.

"Holy—" she started before letting the thought trail off.

Caleb wholeheartedly agreed.

On the wall next to the bed there were cut-out newspaper articles taped across it. Caleb silently scanned them while Jazz went to look in the open closet.

"Delores wrote all of these," Caleb said, voice low. "Not just above-the-fold stories, either."

"If this Jay guy has a thing for Delores, I'm guessing he also has a thing for kerosene."

Caleb looked away from the collage. Jazz pointed to the floor of the closet. Caleb went to her side.

"I know I'm no camping enthusiast but I feel like that's more than what you need for camping," she added.

Caleb crouched down and eyed several containers of kerosene. He cussed.

"You definitely don't need fifteen canisters of it."

Jazz got out her cell phone and started to take pictures. They didn't have a warrant and the excuse they had come inside to make sure no one was in distress would only get them so far. Caleb was careful not to touch anything as he leaned into the closet to make sure he hadn't missed a clue.

The bad feeling he'd had since they walked into the apartment was only growing.

"Let's say Jay DeMarko is our arsonist, triggered by the fire that destroyed his home," Caleb started, rolling forward to the balls of his feet. "He pays Daniel to be a distraction with Nina so he can split our focus. Then, when Daniel comes and sees the kerosene and doesn't believe when Jay says it's for camping supplies, Daniel decides he doesn't want any part of it."

"Then Jay goes and beats the crap out of Daniel to try and shut him up, but Daniel's girlfriend scares him off." Jazz added to the theory. Caleb stood and looked back at the wall and the newspaper articles. Jazz voiced his next question. "But how does Delores fit into this?"

Adrenaline threaded back into Caleb's system.

"She covered his house fire," he said. "She interviewed Angelica and Jay. It was the only article that she wrote about a fire that came *after* one actually happened. It started with her when she wrote that story." He slapped his thigh as more puzzle pieces fit with each other. "And that's why there's a gap in the middle of them all. Delores left town for a year. She didn't write anymore stories. The fires didn't start until she came back and started again."

"Do you think she's in on it, then?"

Caleb shook his head. His gut and her alibis said no. Still, the bad feeling that was growing was reaching an all-time high.

"But I think we need to talk to her. Now."

They rushed out of the apartment and down the stairs to Delores's front door. Caleb didn't have time to curse when they found it was slightly open. He shouldered in and immediately tensed.

The neat living room was trashed. The couch was overturned, a lamp was shattered and the coffee table was cracked. There was blood on the wall closest to one of the bedroom doors.

Wordlessly Caleb opened the first one. It was a stark contrast to Jay's rooms upstairs. The walls were covered in framed pictures and accolades, knickknacks lined the top of a massive dresser and books were stacked on the nightstand. The closet was open and only held hanging clothes.

They went to the next bedroom. It was set up as an office and had nothing of note. It also didn't have a Delores. Caleb finally spoke.

"Call this in while I call Declan. Something bad happ—"

"Detective Nash?"

The voice was far off but he recognized it.

"Delores?"

"I'm in here!"

They rushed back into the first bedroom. One of the large wardrobe doors opened up. Delores Dearborn spilled out. There was a moment when Caleb and Jazz stared in stunned silence. He knew that fear could give people the power to do things they normally couldn't but Delores stuffing herself into the cabinet was a bit startling. She winced as she rubbed her neck and then elbows. It shook the two detectives out of their temporary awe.

"What happened?" Jazz asked, crouching down to help the woman sit up.

A cursory look showed no outward signs of physical distress, other than being stiff from her position in a confined space.

"I figured no one would think to look in there so I hid. Thank God for ten years of gymnastics."

"Why?" Caleb asked as Jazz helped the woman to her feet. "Did Jay attack you?"

Delores's eyes widened.

"Jay saved me from him."

Caleb and Jazz shared a look.

"From who?"

A look of acute alarm crossed Delores's expression. That's when Caleb realized why nothing had been completely adding up. Why the pieces they had weren't forming a puzzle that made sense.

There was a third man.

Chapter Eighteen

Nina was in the kitchen at the main house when she heard a car speed up the road and then slam on its brakes. She didn't recognize the man behind the wheel but it didn't matter.

She saw the gun in his hand when he stepped out.

The glass she was holding clattered into the sink. Nina ran into the hallway between the kitchen and living room. She hurried to the front door and threw the deadbolt just as a shadow appeared on the other side. She didn't wait around to see if he saw her and hurried through to the living room.

The sheriff had been riding on two days with no rest. The glass breaking in the sink hadn't woken him.

But Nina was going to have to.

There were two large windows in the front of the room. Thankfully the couch Declan was on was facing the opposite direction. Nina hit the floor next to it and hesitated.

She hoped Declan wasn't one of those people who woke up swinging.

The front door knob shook. Then the sound of footsteps moved across the wraparound porch. Another shadow appeared. This time on the hardwood on the other side of the couch.

Nina placed her arms over Declan's chest and stomach. Then she whispered his name next to his ear. The tension was almost instant. His eyes flew open, his nostrils flared and he tried to push her off. Nina fastened her grip across him like two seat belts.

"Shh, Declan it's me," she whispered quickly. "It's Nina."

His eyes swiveled to her, his breathing already fast. Nina bet adrenaline was rocking through him, blasting away the haze of sleep and confusion. He gave her a small nod. She pulled her arms back to her sides.

"There's a man at the window with a gun," she said, voice so low she worried he might not have heard her.

Apparently he had. His eyes roved the floor next to her. She assumed he saw the shadow. His eyes widened.

"Hand me my gun," he said, matching her volume.

Nina did as she was told, gently moving the holstered weapon between the coffee table and the sheriff. She moved back so he had room to crawl to the floor next to her, careful to keep the couch as cover.

"Where's Mom?"

Nina pointed up.

"The attic."

Nina was supposed to be with her but had taken a detour to get more water.

Declan checked his gun. The shadow moved, footfalls going in the opposite direction. She guessed he was headed to the next large window. It belonged to the study.

"Use the stairs, grab Mom and hide," Declan urged her.

Nerves knotted Nina's stomach but she nodded. They moved at the same time but she lost track of what Declan was doing; her mind had zeroed in on one task and one task only. Keep Dorothy safe.

She took the stairs two at a time and hurried across the second floor landing to the small set of stairs at the opposite end that led to the attic. Somehow she managed to stay quiet, at least, enough that when she ran into the room Dorothy looked none the wiser.

The older woman had braided her hair back and donned a worn apron. In one hand she held a duster, in the other a thick binder. When she turned to Nina her expression was nothing but exasperated.

Then it quickly turned to worry.

"There's a man outside with a gun." Nina bowled through. "Declan told me to get you and then hide."

Bless her, Dorothy didn't hesitate.

She put down what she was holding and motioned for Nina to follow her.

"I've got a gun in my bedroom," she said as she passed.

Nina felt a small amount of relief at that. At least they wouldn't be defenseless if anything happened to—

A gunshot and glass shattering imploded the silent urgency around them. Dorothy stumbled backward on the landing. For one terrifying moment Nina thought she'd been the one shot. She wrapped her arms around the woman to steady her.

The second, third and fourth shots went off next. Each one made them both jump where they stood. A loud bang followed, shaking the floor slightly. Nina guessed someone had thrown open the front door. She tried to push Dorothy into moving but was met with surprising resistance.

That's when she realized what had the woman grounded.

Her son might be hurt. Or worse.

The fact that the shooting had stopped and Declan wasn't calling for them was more than gut wrenching.

But Nina had to keep Dorothy safe. They couldn't help Declan any more than they could help themselves if they were targeted next.

"We need your gun," Nina reminded the woman, whispering next to her ear.

Instead of pushing Dorothy, Nina moved around her and pulled her along, heading for the room she assumed belonged to the matriarch. It wasn't an easy task but Dorothy seemed to limber up once they had crossed the threshold into a room that Nina would have admired in any other situation.

"It's in my nightstand."

Dorothy pointed to the one she meant and turned to face the door. Nina hustled, every second without any sounds from downstairs grating against her skin. The gun was there, like Dorothy said. Nina didn't know much about them but knew just because it was small and fit easily in her palm didn't mean it wouldn't do a good amount of damage.

Nina went and grabbed Dorothy's hand. She pulled the older woman to the closet. It was a large walk-in. Stacks of luggage along one of the walls made the perfect place to hide. She started to say as much when a man shouting met their ears.

And it wasn't Declan.

"Nina Drake, if you don't come down here right now I'll kill the sheriff."

Nina froze.

Dorothy didn't.

She started forward, not even bothering to ask for the gun.

"Wait," Nina insisted.

"He's got my baby!"

Dorothy had such a fierce look in her eyes, Nina knew then there was nothing she could say to stop the woman. No matter that he'd asked for Nina and not her. No matter that they didn't even know if Declan was still alive. No matter that the angry man might just kill anyone who walked down the stairs.

No, Dorothy was going to go save her son no matter what.

So Nina made a decision right then and there.

Her mother had been killed by senseless anger. She wasn't going to let Caleb's mother suffer the same fate.

"Let me go first," she said, fear releasing its hold long enough for her to form a plan. "He asked for me. Here, you can take the gun and watch my back."

Dorothy's maternal rage saw sense in that. She took

the handgun and let Nina leave the closet first. A choice she was about to regret.

Nina whirled around and shut the closet door in Dorothy's face. She pushed her hip against the wood while reaching for the nightstand next to it. The piece of furniture was heavy, not cheap. Nina barely managed to pull it close enough to wedge it against the door.

"Nina," Dorothy warned through it.

"I'll save Declan," she said right back. "I need you to be safe."

Nina didn't wait around to discuss it any further. She left the room and made it to the stairs.

"You better not be doing anything dumb," the voice warned from the first floor, close enough that Nina knew he was near the foot of the stairs. From this angle she couldn't see his face. Or Declan's. "That includes having a weapon. If I see anything, I'm going to kill both of you and then go hunting for the Nash mother. Got it?"

"I'm unarmed," she promised. "I'm coming down now."

Her legs shook but Nina slowly descended, arms raised to prove she wasn't holding anything. It wasn't until her shoes hit the hardwood floor that the reasons she hadn't wanted Dorothy to come down really sank in.

A man she didn't recognize stepped into view from the living room. Tall, lanky, young. His hair was pulled back in a low ponytail and his dark eyes were blazing with defiance. He had a gun pointed at her.

"Glad to finally meet the infamous Nina Drake,"

he said, sounding not at all glad. "I've heard so much about you, but I'm afraid we're going to have skip the talking and leave. You first."

He motioned to the front door. It was off its hinges, the glass portion now scattered along the floor. Nina took a breath and walked across it to the front porch.

"Who are you and where's—" she started but then gasped. "Declan!"

On the porch, outside of what had once been the living room window, was the sheriff. He was lying on his side, eyes closed, blood collecting across his shirt.

"He's not dead, just shot," the man said at her back. "But I'll make sure he's dead right now if you don't help me get him into the car. We're kind of on a time-line right now."

Nina didn't question him, especially after she confirmed Declan was, in fact, still breathing. He'd been shot in the shoulder and stirred as they struggled to lift and then drag him to the car. A feat in itself, given how large the man was. Nina slid into the back seat with him, refusing to leave his side. The gunman got into the front and started the engine.

"Put pressure on it," he commanded, voice tight. Nina raised her eyebrow. He saw it in the rearview. "Put pressure on the wound to help stop the bleeding."

Nina was about to question why the man had given her the advice when he'd been the one who created the wound in the first place, but their attention flew to a second car racing their way. The man cussed something awful and tried to peel out. The other car didn't want that.

It slammed into them.

Nina didn't have time to yell. She tried her best to keep Declan from flying out of his seat. A warm wetness pressed against her face as she wedged her body between the sheriff and the front seats. Their captor strung together several not-so-great words again. He stopped the car, flung open his door and then opened the one behind her. Nina couldn't scramble away from his grip. He grabbed the back of her shirt and pulled.

"Let go," he ground out when Nina refused to move. "Let go or I'll shoot him in the head."

Nina didn't want to but she believed the man. She let go and was yanked right out of the car. The man kept his grip on the back of her shirt. He didn't move them, though. Instead, his attention was on the driver of the car that had just hit them.

"You did this to yourself," he yelled out. "You went after mine so I went after yours!"

The car door opened but before the newcomer stepped out he had a word of warning.

"If you hurt her, I'll kill you."

The voice was low yet booming.

And familiar.

"You need me," her captor replied with vehemence. He shook his grip. Nina winced at the movement, her nerves more than shot at this point. "So let us leave."

The man behind the wheel of the other car slowly got out.

He was grinning.

The man at her back readjusted his grip on her shirt

to around her neck. It forced her head to tilt back, but
she still could see the man across from them.

Every part of Nina split in two.

Half was in the present.

The air had cooled because of the impending storm.
She smelled the promise of rain on the breeze and the
sweet smell of Dorothy's blooming flowers from her
garden just beneath it. She could see the ranch and its
green grass, bountiful trees and beautiful fields stretching out all around them. She could feel the dirt displac-
ing beneath her shoe as the man behind her forced her
to change her stance to keep steady.

The other half of her was in a much different place.

The asphalt burned her bare feet, her flip-flops long
abandoned. The smell of the sea mixed with the wind
that gently blew across the trees next to her. An acrid
smell of burning metal was cloying.

A boy had his arms around her, a weight that kept
her tethered to a world that was burning in front of her.

And there was that smile.

His father, staring at the wreckage, like he didn't
have a care in the world.

Then, all at once, the past and the present collided.

Thanks to that same smile.

This time, it was worn by the son.

Jeremy Bowling met her gaze without any surprise
whatsoever. He even gave her a small nod of hello.

"Nina, why don't you come over here?" he said,
patting his hand against his leg like she was a dog.
The man who had a grip on her neck didn't want her
to comply to the new command.

"If you even think about it I'll kill the sheriff," he seethed. Jeremy heard the threat. He tilted his head to the side, looking into the back of their car.

"You're using the eldest Nash to control her," he stated analytically. His eyes roamed back to hers. "I'm surprised it works, to be honest."

With a speed that didn't seem possible, Jeremy pulled his gun up and shot. Nina didn't have time to scream. She didn't have time to even move. The hand around her neck loosened and then the pressure was gone. Shaking like a leaf, Nina chanced a look behind her.

The man fell to the ground. His eyes were wide. He looked down at the bullet wound in his chest.

Footsteps crunched across the dirt, coming closer. Nina cursed herself for not scooping up the gun when she had the chance. Jeremy appeared at her shoulder, so close she could smell the spice of aftershave.

"Maybe you are a good girl, after all."

Nina opened her mouth but, like the shot, Jeremy was once again painfully fast.

The blow against her head knocked Nina out cold.

Chapter Nineteen

The throbbing of pain let Nina know she was alive. That was her first thought. It wasn't as comforting as it should have been.

Pain pulsed along every blink as she clawed her way out of unconsciousness. A gray room materialized through the fog, filled with odd, dingy white shapes. It took longer than it should have to realize they were pieces of furniture covered in sheets.

Nina was tied to a chair among them.

She turned her head to try and see behind her. The moan that escaped happened before she could stop it. Pain stabbed at her so quickly, the wave of nausea that followed nearly overwhelmed her. She closed her eyes tight and took long breaths. Waking up in a room she didn't recognize, alone and bound to a chair, wasn't a good situation. She didn't want to add getting sick all over herself to that list.

The urge to vomit lessened. The pain didn't. Nina took the small win and, this time, slowly turned her head. A window was set at the back of the room. She only saw dark skies.

"Not helpful," she grumbled.

Next she tested her restraints. Rope dug into her wrists behind the chair. There was no leeway. No give. Jeremy had done more than a great job at that.

Jeremy.

Nina didn't say the name out loud, but after she thought it a shiver ran through her.

His last words before he knocked her unconscious had rooted themselves in her memory. They echoed the email Daniel Covington had sent.

And everyone thought you were a nice girl.

Maybe you are a nice girl, after all.

Jeremy had been behind the email, she was sure of it, but why? And who was the man who had shot Declan? And where was the sheriff?

Fear was an emotion she was becoming desensitized to at this point, confusion and frustration not so much.

Why was Jeremy in Overlook?

What did he want from her?

A pang of longing nearly brought that fear to a new level, one where she could feel it again. Just last night she'd let her guard down and gotten close with Caleb. Sharing the burdens of their pasts had done more for her heart than she ever thought it would. Sharing that burden with Caleb had done even more.

Yet she'd never thought her burden, her past, would put him and his family in danger.

Nina moved her feet around, testing the restraints at her ankles. Surprisingly they weren't as tight as the rope around her wrists. She pushed out her feet in opposite directions. The knot on top seemed to loosen.

A flash of hope burned through her.

She did the same thing again but moved each foot to a different spot before pushing out. The rope became more slack. She continued, rotating where she pushed out on the rope each time until it finally came untied.

Riding another jolt of adrenaline, Nina rocked forward and stood, thankful the chair was of the dining variety and not something clunky like a lounger. It was an awkward move but after a few moments she managed to steady herself, despite being hunched over.

Then she had to look around the room.

If she had to guess she was in an attic of some sort, much like the one at the ranch's main house. There were no closets, only one light that hung in the middle of the room, and in between the pieces of furniture were several boxes labeled with names like Christmas, Halloween and Rider's Graduation. Nina went to the Christmas box and set her chair down. With her feet she tried to finagle the box open.

It didn't work.

She gave up and went to the closest sheet, sat down and pulled it off. Beneath it was a wide and narrow bookcase Short, too. The edge of it was just the right height.

Nina stood and turned around again. She stifled a yelp as she lost her balance and collided with the floor. Unable to stop herself, her face took the brunt of the fall. She almost got sick again as a new source of pain exploded along her right brow. Warmth immediately slid across her skin.

Nina didn't have time to writhe in her mistake.

Wherever Jeremy was, if he was in the house he would have heard that.

She struggled back up to her feet and moved as close as she could to get the rope at her wrists near the edge of the piece of furniture. It looked like it was handmade, the top piece one long plank of stained wood. Its edge was what Nina was placing all of her hope on. It looked sharp, despite the rest of it seeming worn.

Whatever Jeremy had planned for her, it was nothing good.

A few minutes went by but no one came to the door. Nina was counting that blessing as she sawed. At first she felt like a fool, doubting she was doing anything at all, but then the tension in the ropes lessened. It encouraged a more ferocious approach. Her legs burned and trembled as she supported the weight of the chair while hunching over so the ropes would meet the edge. Still, she didn't stop. When the rope was finally slack enough to give her confidence, Nina sat back down. She took a steadying breath and then pulled as hard as she could.

Feeling that rope break was better than sex. Or, at least, a close second.

She brought her hands in front of her and shed the rest of her bindings. Then she moved to the one around her waist. It was tied on the side but not impossible to unknot. She hurried through it, ignoring the stinging in her eye that was only getting worse. Once she was completely untethered from the dining chair she wiped the blood from her brow and crept to the window.

Finally Nina knew something.

Looking down and into the distance she spotted the familiar river where there used to be a bridge.

Overlook Pass, she thought with more excitement than it probably warranted to finally know at least one part of the situation. Which meant she was in the house that was just behind it. The owner had moved to be with her daughter, according to Caleb.

She scanned the room again with new attention. Nothing just screamed out weapon. She ended up going through most of the boxes, hoping the owner had labeled them incorrectly. Nina imagined a box full of guns that could help her defend herself hidden in a box that said University Things.

Nina decided to not waste any more time. She didn't even take a deep breath before she was opening the door as slowly as if a sleeping baby were right next to it. The motion was easy but a low squeak sounded. Nina bit her lip and opened it far enough that she could slide through.

Like she'd suspected, she was in an attic much like Dorothy's. It opened into a slightly different layout but the important aspect was the same. She was on the second floor and the stairs were right in front of her. Theoretically she was closer to freedom than she had been. Two doors were on either side of the landing. Both were closed.

Declan.

What if Jeremy had taken him and he was tied to a chair in one of the other rooms?

Nina thought of Caleb and his obvious love for his family. It put the fire of courage in her belly, calming her quaking limbs. She hadn't even realized she'd been shaking.

The first room was much like the attic. Things were boxed up, furniture was covered by drop cloths. There was no Declan. The second room was a bit trickier. The door was locked.

Nina froze for a moment, worried she'd alert Jeremy if he was on the other side. When nothing happened she pressed her ear against the door, hoping to hear the sheriff.

She was both relieved and disappointed. It was nice not to hear a man tied up and in pain but there was no guarantee he would be making any noise. The last time she saw him he'd been unconscious.

Which brought her to the top of the stairs.

Nina bit her lip again.

Her head was throbbing. Her face was bleeding. The closer she came to escaping, the more she realized Jeremy could be waiting for her downstairs. What did he want?

This time anger came to the forefront of the emotional gauntlet she seemed to have been running for the last two days. It cut through her nerves and worries and she hurried down the stairs, trying her best to be quiet while also ready to turn her walk into an all-out run for her life if necessary.

Once she was off the last step she took that energy and spun around to look down the hallway. It seemed to run through the middle of the house, ending at the back door. The urge to run burned across the soles of her feet but she refused to leave Declan. If something happened to him, she would never forgive herself.

She crept along the hallway, pausing to listen every few steps. It felt like just an empty old house. Had Jeremy left her there? What was the plan?

The kitchen, former dining room and living room were empty. No boxes, no furniture with sheets. No signs of anyone else. Did that mean Declan could be upstairs?

If Jeremy wasn't in the house then surely she could go back and try to open the locked room without being caught, right?

Nina was about to turn around when a crack of thunder made her gasp. Like a scene from a horror movie, the back door opened. The man in its frame was for the briefest of seconds draped in shadows, blackened skies his backdrop.

Jeremy's eyes widened a moment then he smiled.

"I was about to come get you but this saves me a trip up the stairs."

Nina backpedaled so hard she almost toppled over. However, she refused to be the woman in most of those same horror movies who fell when she was being chased by the bad guy.

Yet Jeremy didn't make one move.

He didn't have to.

"You run, I kill Declan," he said simply.

Nina froze, eyes now on the front door. On freedom.

"I won't chase you," he added, voice nothing but conversational.

"What do you want, Jeremy?" she asked, her voice low and angry. "What could you possibly want?"

Nina turned back to face him. His smile was gone. Somehow that was more unsettling.

"I want to talk and then I want you to make a decision."

CALEB WAS SPITTING MAD. Hell, he was more than spitting. There was blood on the ground outside of the main house and not just in one spot. It started on the front porch, across the shattered living room window glass, and continued into the dirt. Then it disappeared, along with whatever car had been hit by the one he and Jazz had seen when they drove up.

Though that detail hadn't filtered in as fast since his mama was hanging over Jay DeMarko's prone body, cell phone on the dirt next to her, gun clearly sticking out of her apron pocket and hands covered in blood as she applied pressure to Jay's gunshot wound.

"I called the department because your phone was busy," his mother yelled as soon as he was out of the truck. Jazz was right behind him, pulling up in Delores's SUV. They hadn't wanted to leave her alone but hadn't had the time to wait for a deputy or to take her to the department themselves.

"I was calling you," he yelled, adrenaline making him lose control of his volume. Neither Nina nor Declan had answered so his mother had been his next call. Her phone had been busy. Now he knew why.

"After I broke down my own closet door I called an ambulance and Chief Deputy Murdock," she kept on, eyes wild.

Caleb came to her side but didn't remove his hand from his gun. Now he had more information. Jay wasn't the only man he had to worry about. Yet his mother let him know with one look that the threat was gone.

And the woman threatened with him.

What he didn't know was another kick to the gut.

"Caleb, a man took Nina and Declan." The look that accompanied that bad news was darker than the sky ever would be. "And I think Declan was shot." Caleb felt himself shift into work mode, detaching from the emotions broiling in his chest.

There was hell to pay and he couldn't afford to make any mistakes.

Chapter Twenty

"I met Jeremy when he moved upstairs." Delores stood at the head of the dining room table, chin up and voice strong. "We hit it off immediately and I even became friends with Jay. He seemed normal enough and Jeremy, well, he seemed perfect. I suppose that might have been on purpose now. He just had an answer for everything...until he didn't."

She directed her gaze at Caleb. Jazz stood at his side. His mother had gone to the hospital with a deputy and Jay at Caleb's insistence. Chief Deputy Murdock was leading the charge across the county to try and find Nina, Declan and Jeremy. Since every second counted, Caleb had been authorized to do a more pointed search, running down whatever leads Delores might be able to give them.

Not that he'd asked permission.

"When you showed up asking about the articles I wrote and the fires, I genuinely had no idea if or how they were important. Until you mentioned your house fire had been started by fireworks," she continued. "See, Jeremy and I never hung out at his apartment. He said he liked mine better since he hadn't had a chance to decorate his yet. But the week before you showed up I tried to bring him some dinner. The door was unlocked because he'd gone down to the mailboxes. I went into his room to see if he was there but found a bag of fireworks instead. I thought it might have been a romantic surprise but when I asked him about it he gave me the oddest answer. He said it was a means to an end and none of my business."

Her jaw set.

"No one condescends to me without a fight. So I started digging. I looked past his Facebook and called a friend and finally found a news story about him. And Nina. I knew it couldn't be a coincidence that, after all these years, both of them wound up in small-town Overlook, Tennessee. Then I remembered what I'd heard about Claire and the new girl in town teaming up to take down Daniel Covington. I know his girlfriend so I called and she said he'd been released from jail. So then I called him and said if he was connected to Jeremy or Jay and knew anything about the fires or Nina he better come clean. Daniel may be full of himself half of the time, but he genuinely seemed to have no idea what I was talking about."

She managed to look sheepish. "Honestly, I was feeling so silly about it then, thinking I'd jumped to conclusions. So I was going to wait and call you in the morning—this morning—but then Jay woke me up."

There was no denying the fear that skated across Delores's expression at the memory.

"I never really talked to him but when he told me

that I needed to hide because Jeremy was coming, I believed him with all of my heart. I ran into the bedroom, thanked God my Grandma Tildy gave me her larger-than-life wardrobe and stuffed myself into one of its cabinets. No sooner had I shut the door than they started fighting in the living room. I couldn't make out what they were saying in the scuffle but they both cut out of there quick. You showed up shortly after. And that's all I know."

"You're who Daniel was talking about," Caleb said thoughtfully. "When he said, 'but then she called.' I think you're right. I don't think he had a clue about the fires. I think he went and confronted Jay and Jeremy and found the kerosene. Decided he didn't want any part of it. Jeremy or Jay found out and one of them tried to end him but his girlfriend spooked them before they could finish the job." Caleb refrained from adding *then Jeremy went to try and end you*, but by the look in her eyes, Delores had already put that together.

"We can get into the specifics later," Jazz intervened. "We know Jay doesn't have Declan and Nina, Jeremy does. We know, based on what you told us, Caleb, that Jeremy probably wants some kind of revenge for her testimony against his father, but where would he do it? And how? I hate to say it, but if he'd wanted both of them dead he could have done it easily right here."

Caleb didn't like that thought, though he knew it was true.

"Why did he go through all of whatever it is he did

when it would have been much simpler and less risky to just grab her? Or, well, kill her."

"He has to make it dramatic."

Caleb was sure of it the moment it came out.

Realization lit up Jazz's expression.

"Because the trial was."

Caleb nodded. "Not only was his father facing prison and then sentenced, but it was turned into a spectacle. Some of the media even called the outcome poetic." He balled his fists in anger. "The pictures taken of Nina here were all of her smiling. A smile was what doomed his father. The smile she saw but he didn't. It's not just enough for Jeremy to win, he has to do it in style for it to count."

"That theory makes sense," Delores said. "Almost like an eye for an eye."

"How do the fires figure into this? He's trying to recreate the actual event?" Jazz paused before she said the next part. "Trapping her in a car and setting it on fire?"

They all quieted as they thought. Caleb pushed past his rage again. He didn't need the distraction right—

"Distractions," he said, more to himself. The one word sent a series of thoughts tumbling. "Jeremy has been in town for months, masterminding some kind of finale. We might have messed that up but he's not just going to scrap everything. Now, why would a man that dedicated and clever team up with someone like Jay DeMarko? An arsonist. Starting a fire isn't hard." He knew he must have looked crazed when he spoke next but his gut was finally syncing up with his head.

"What are fires, Jazz?" Her eyebrow quirked up. He answered before she could. "They're dangerous, hard-to-miss, distracting."

"So you think he only used Jay to keep our attention on Jay."

"And Daniel Covington," Caleb reminded her. "We didn't even know there was a third guy and might not have if it wasn't for Delores."

Delores didn't comment on the compliment. Instead she voiced her own question.

"If he's not going to mirror what happened to Nina's mother then maybe he doesn't have a set pathology. Maybe he doesn't need to be that dramatic."

"You don't go through this much trouble just to smear the details at the end," Caleb said, sure in his words. He rubbed his jaw. Another uncomfortable thought pushed its way through. "Nina said that smoke inhalation was what killed her mother. But that's not true." Both women raised their eyebrows in question. "She was trapped. That's what really killed her. That's what sealed her fate. And Jeremy's father didn't try to save her."

"But where would Jeremy try to trap her?" Delores asked.

Caleb's mind was racing.

"If he was using an arsonist as a distraction, then maybe he'd get his revenge in the last place we would think to look for one."

NINA LOOKED FROM the car down to the river. Her wrists were now tied behind her back and she was terrified.

"I thought you wanted to talk," she reminded Jeremy. He had walked her at gunpoint from the abandoned house's back door to where the Overlook Pass bridge had once been. Together they now stood at the river, Nina so close to the edge the temptation to leap in swayed through her while Jeremy kept his distance. The car she'd originally been forced into was parked a few feet from them, facing the water. Nina's heart squeezed as she saw Declan hunched over in the back seat.

Jeremy didn't make any assurances that talking was the only topic on the agenda. Instead, he jumped into a story that hardened his gaze and felt more than rehearsed.

"I see the way you look at me," he started. "You're trying to figure out if I've always been crazy or if it's a more recent development. Why am I in Overlook? Why did I abduct you? Why, why, why. The truth is, I'm not crazy, which honestly is worse, I think. I'm smart, hardworking and no stranger to sacrifice. I'm a trifecta, Nina. One this little town never stood a chance against." He smirked. "But why, the little girl thought?" he added, adopting an almost whimsical tone. Nina found it more frightening than if he had been yelling.

His smirk was wiped clean by practiced indifference.

"You know, I didn't think about you for a few years. I actually did quite well for myself. I'd always had an interest in the medical field but figured out that the mind is a much more challenging beast to tame. So I became a psychiatrist. I went to college on an academic scholarship, graduated with an MD, completed a quite grueling residency and then joined a psychiatry practice where everyone called me Doctor Bowling. It reminded me of all the things I'd gained. And then my father died in prison."

Nina was speechless on more than one account. Jeremy was right. She had assumed he was crazy, imaging a young boy warping into a disturbed man. But a psychiatrist?

And his father had died?

How had she missed that information? The local media had proven to be sharks when it came to the trial. Surely they would have used his death to rehash it.

"Not many people know," he said, picking up on her thoughts. "His suicide wasn't tantalizing enough. The money I spread around to keep it quiet helped, too, I'm sure."

"I'm sorry." Nina meant it, even if she would never forgive the eldest Bowling. Still, losing a parent was heartbreaking, especially when they didn't die naturally.

Jeremy gave her a critical eye, then nodded.

"Do you know he was one of the only two living relatives I had? After the trial I was shipped off to his mother's. I don't think I'll ever meet someone as horrible as her. She didn't care for my father and she only cared to yell at me. When she died the world became a brighter place. I was finally free of all the bad." There was a fire in his eyes. Nina wondered how his grandmother died but didn't want to interrupt his speech. Every moment they kept talking was another moment given to Caleb and the department to try and find them. Nina didn't know how long she'd been unconscious. She wanted to make sure she stalled as long as she could.

Plus, Jeremy had an intriguing air about him. He was oddly captivating when he spoke. Nina assumed that was thanks to his profession.

"But when Dad died, I realized freedom and escape were illusions I'd made to cope with my grief. That there was a truth I'd been avoiding for years." He lowered the gun. Somehow it made him appear far more menacing. "You, Nina Drake. You lied. My father never smiled."

Nina broke through her decision to keep quiet.

"He was smiling, Jeremy," she said, voice low but strong. "I saw him. He was standing there and—"

"He said it was an accident," Jeremy roared.

Nina flinched but refused to cower.

"He hit the car on the purpose," she shot back. "The investigation showed that he didn't once hit the brakes! You were in the car! Did it seem like an accident?"

Jeremy's face reddened in anger.

"I never saw him smile!"

"But he did!"

Jeremy brought the gun up and shook it. He took a step closer. This time Nina did move backward.

"Shut up," he seethed. "You lied! I saved you and how do you repay me?" Nina couldn't step back any farther without falling off of the ledge and into the water. She had nowhere to go as Jeremy moved so close to her that she felt his breath against her face as he yelled. "You lie! You lied to the cops, you lied on the stand, and worst of all, to everyone you became the hero!"

He pushed the gun to her chest and used his other hand to point to himself.

"I was the hero!"

Nina feared that this was it. That she had run out of time. Whatever poise Jeremy had possessed was clearly gone.

What did they say about reasoning with a madman? Don't.

Nina kept quiet, her heart hammering in her chest.

Finally the heat behind Jeremy's eyes seemed to cool. He lowered the gun and actually laughed.

"Now it's time to go."

He stepped back and motioned to the car.

"What?"

He continued to point.

"Go to the car now and get into the driver's seat or I'll go kill the sheriff."

The space between the riverbank and the car seemed dreadfully long. And it felt too much like a dead man's march.

"So you're going to kill us?" She chanced the question as she reached the door. He still had his gun trained on her. "As punishment for what you believe?"

He cracked a smile that in every way was opposite of the ones Caleb had given her. The detective's were warm, kind and compassionate. Jeremy's were twisted and menacing, and promised pain.

"I'm going to give my father justice by showing you

the truly bad intentions you made others believe he had that day." He glanced at the water. "This is the deepest part of the river for miles and miles. I convinced Jay to hone his arson's method on the bridge that used to be here so there would be enough room." His twisted smile stretched. "You're going to drive this car right into it, where you'll then sink to the bottom and become trapped."

Nina's blood froze.

"Why would I do that?" she asked, unable to stop the waver that broke through. "Why wouldn't I just let you shoot me now?"

Jeremy pointed to the backseat.

"Because of him," he said of Declan. "If you drive the two of you into the water there's a high chance you'll both drown. But if you don't there's a one hundred percent chance he will receive a bullet to the head and then I'll simply throw you in the car myself to get the job done. Now, get in the car or—" he moved so his aim was on Declan's unconscious form "—the sheriff never wakes up again."

Nina nodded that she understood. Jeremy opened the car door and let her maneuver into the driver's seat. He put the car in Drive.

"Not only am I smart, Nina, I'm an excellent shot, even with moving targets," he said. "All you will do is floor it, and gravity and inertia will do the rest. Anything else and you'll just drown with a corpse."

Nina felt sick to her stomach.

"This won't change anything," she said. "This won't bring either of our parents back."

Jeremy shook his head.

"What you don't understand Nina, is that I know people. I know what they're thinking. In hindsight you would have died, too, that day, trying to save your mother. You're only here now because I saved you. Now I'm correcting the mistake. *We're* correcting a mistake."

Jeremy started to shut the door but paused. He had one last dramatic parting shot.

"And then, while you're drowning down there, do you know what I'll do, daughter of the victim?"

She didn't respond.

She already knew the answer.

"I'll. Just. Smile."

Chapter Twenty-One

Nina thought they would be okay. At least, she had hope still as they started to sink. She guessed the water was around twelve-feet deep, maybe more. The drop to meet it she hadn't been nearly as far. All the windows were up which meant they would hopefully just go to the bottom and sit there, giving Caleb and company more time to find them. At least she hoped that was what might happen. In truth she had no idea what to do. She also hoped the man who attacked them at the main house, who she guessed was their arsonist, had survived and told Caleb everything. Including where this plan had ended. Though, as the water rose above the door handles just outside, Nina made another guess.

Their arsonist hadn't been in the loop.

Which meant there might not be any bread crumbs to follow to save her and Declan.

Those weren't happy thoughts to have but, again, she still had hope as the windows were covered by a brilliant, cool blue.

But then the water started coming in.

Declan groaned, bringing Nina fresh relief, until she saw what had stirred him.

The window behind his head was cracked open and water was coming in fast. On reflex Nina tried to angle her hands to the power window controls but nothing happened. She let out an anguished cry. Now their hope of sitting at the bottom of the river was gone. Now they had until the water filled the car.

"Declan?"

The sheriff's eyes opened slowly, water spilling down his shoulder. Nina did an awkward scurry over through the middle of the seats until she was falling against the man.

"What's going on?" he managed, catching her.

Nina could have sung for joy in an instant.

"Untie my hands," she yelled.

Bless him, the sheriff immediately went into action. The power in the car cut out. The light outside was fading as the water poured in.

Her bonds loosened and fell away. Nina immediately turned and helped Declan move as far away from the water as the back seat allowed. The movement came along with a string of moans from the man. When he spoke again his voice was dangerously weak.

"When—when the water gets to your chin you—you might be to open the door. If not, wait. It'll pressurize when it's—when it's full" He started to fall over. Nina used her position against the door to wrap her arms around him, letting her chest hold up his back.

"Then we'll swim out," she said defiantly.

He was barely able to shake his head.

"Leave me."

"I'm not leaving you, Declan. Do you hear me? I am not letting you die down here."

Nina waited for his retort. Instead his body went limp against her. The added weight was surprising. It pinned her against the door.

Declan remained silent.

The darkness was a terrifying companion to the rising water. Nina should have been scared, and yet her body was calm.

And she had Caleb Nash to thank for that.

She hadn't known the man for long but knew one thing was certain. He would fight to his very last breath to save the ones he loved.

Which was exactly what she was going to do for him.

She pressed one hand against Declan's gunshot wound and waited. If she couldn't get out when it got to their heads then she'd have to get them out as fast as possible when the inside was completely flooded.

There were no other options.

The cold from the river wrapped itself around her, crawling higher and higher.

"Easy peasy."

CALEB HAULED ASS to the Overlook Pass. He didn't even slow down as he rounded the house that stood sentry across from it. He didn't even reduce speed when Jeremy Bowling raised his gun and started shooting.

In fact, what Caleb felt was an overwhelming amount of relief. He had been operating under a theory, a hunch. One that could have been devastatingly off. Yet, there Jeremy was, standing by the river.

That relief fell as fast as Caleb's stomach did.

The river.

Caleb took a sharp turn and hit the brakes. He jumped out shooting, using his car as cover. Jazz and Delores were right behind. There was nowhere for Jeremy to run and hide now.

He took three bullets to the middle before he dropped his gun. Caleb was running to the riverbank before Jeremy's body hit the ground.

"In the water," he yelled back as soon as he saw the distorted darkness at the bottom of the water and bubbles coming to the surface.

Caleb dropped his gun and took a running jump. He dove in headfirst, Jazz yelling behind him.

The water was cold. It would have been a shock to his system had his blood not been coursing with full-blown adrenaline. He pumped his legs and arms and descended into the darkness. It wasn't until he was a few feet from the car that he saw the terrifying sight.

The back door was open. One body was floating outside of it. Caleb didn't have time to sort through the terrible thoughts before movement caught his eye. The body outside of the car was Declan's, the one moving next to him was Nina. Her eyes widened as he reached them. She didn't waste any time. She pointed to Declan and then up to the surface. She even gave him a push.

Caleb realized then Declan's eyes were closed. It tore at his heart. Nina pointed again. Caleb looped his arm around his brother and used the car's hood to push off. They soared through the water. Two splashes displaced the area next to them as they broke the surface. Jazz was already reaching for Declan, Delores at his side.

"Help me get him to the bank over there," Jazz yelled. Delores followed directions. They pulled Declan from his arms.

"Where's Nina?"

Caleb turned, expecting to see her break the surface next to him and smile.

But she didn't.

Caleb dove back under, heart two seconds from breaking loose and going to get her itself, and swam the fastest he ever had back to the car. Nina was still moving but she wasn't going anywhere. Her foot was caught on something in the car.

Caleb reached down to her ankle. The seat belt had tangled around her. He reached for the knife in his pocket, thankful his dad had passed on the tradition to him. Nina's hand gripped his shoulder.

Then that grip loosened altogether.

He sawed through the belt with added ferocity. When it gave he grabbed her and pushed off the top of the car for the second time. Again, he soared through the water.

Again, the person he was holding wasn't moving.

Stay with me, Nina.

Please.

RAIN.

Nina heard it before she saw it.

"Oh! You're waking up!"

Nina's eyelids felt woefully heavy. They fought her and gravity as she tried to open them. By the time she did the voice was much closer—one she didn't recognize but was, at the same time, familiar.

"Hi there," said the woman. She wore a floral-patterned dress with a blazer and had a braid running over her shoulder. Her hair was an exact match for Caleb's, just as her smile was. A small but noticeable scar ran across her left cheekbone.

"You're Madi," Nina guessed. The woman nodded.

"The best of the siblings, in my opinion," she joked. "But I can talk more about that later. Right now I bet my last dollar that you have some questions. First, though, how are you feeling? What's the last thing you remember?"

Nina blinked a few times as if the movement could pull out her memories. They came slowly.

"I was in the car at the bottom of the river," she started. "Declan told me to wait until the water got to our chins or flooded the inside to try and open the door and leave him, but I told him no." Madi's expression softened. "I got the door open and was going to push him out with me." Nina remembered the seat belt then. She glanced down at her ankle. All she saw were white sheets. She realized with a start that she was in the hospital. "When I was trying to get Declan out I got caught in the seat belt. It—it startled me and I lost some of the breath I was holding. Then I saw Caleb." Madi's pleasant smile took on an unmistakable mask of pride. "I told him to take Declan up. Then I remember he came back. Then I couldn't breathe."

Madi reached out and patted Nina's hand with reassurance.

"From what I've been told, Caleb pulled you out and gave you CPR on the riverbank after you surfaced. You coughed up water and started breathing again but had a hard time waking up." Madi motioned around the room. "The doctor said it was exhaustion. From what I was told, you had quite an intense past few days."

Nina nodded. Adrenaline and stress had been hard enough. Add in drowning and she could see how her body decided to take a sabbatical.

"How's Declan?" Nina asked, guilt pooling in her stomach. She should have asked about him first.

Madi's smile broke a little but she answered without pause.

"It was very touch-and-go at the beginning but he's hanging in there," she said. "He might not be a part of our triplet bond but I can feel it in my bones that he'll come through this. If there was one thing he got from our father it's an unwavering stubbornness."

Nina felt a weight lift in relief. Then she was looking around the room for his brother. Madi seemed to pick up on it. Her smile was whole again.

"It was hard to get Caleb to leave your side," she offered. "But he knew your father would have questions so he and Des went to go get him from the airport."

Nina almost sat all the way up.

"My dad?"

Madi nodded.

"Let this be the first lesson you learn about life on the ranch—when one of us gets hurt, we all get hurt. We're all family. Nothing stops us from making sure we're all okay. That includes calling in dads when their only child gets targeted by a madman."

Days ago Nina would have argued, would have groaned at the idea, but now she found she didn't have the heart to do it. In fact, she realized a visit from her dad, even with the stress of what had happened attached, might do her heart some good. She'd been living so long with it locked up, it sure needed some fresh air. Though mention of a madman brought her to the next series of questions.

"What happened to Jeremy?"

This time Madi hesitated.

"I'll give you the bare bones of what I know but the rest you should get from Caleb. I think he's still putting it together. But what I *do* know is that Jeremy was killed in the firefight next to the river. Caleb and Jazz defended themselves and then immediately went into the water."

Nina didn't know how to feel about Jeremy's death. Relief wasn't the right word; sadness wasn't either. It was something she would, no doubt, think about for a long time to come.

"Now that we got that out of the way, I have to ask you a personal question," Madi continued. "If that's alright with you."

Nina found herself nodding. She liked Madi already.

"So, Mom told me in the hallway before Caleb left that *she* thinks you two have kissed and I am trying my hardest not to be nosy but—" Madi stopped mid-thought and busted out laughing. Nina's cheeks were warm and she was smiling like a schoolgirl. "Just a word of advice—when this all settles down and Mom comes at you with relationship questions, you might want to work on your poker face."

Nina couldn't help it. She laughed.

Chapter Twenty-Two

Nina found him at the fence line closest to where his house used to be. His horse, Ax, was roaming next to him while the man sat on the posts, gaze sweeping over the debris that used to be his home. Nina felt her heart squeeze. Part of it was sympathy for the man, most of it was just because of the man in general.

"Hey there," she called. Caleb looked over his shoulder and graced her with one of his famous smiles. He started to get down but Nina shook her head. "I'll join you."

She set the big bag she'd been carrying against the wooden fence as he helped her up and over the top. For a moment they were quiet. Nina took in a deep, cleansing breath and let it out. Caleb was still smiling. She still marveled over how their silence was always companionable.

"I just came back from dropping Dad off at the airport," she said after a while. "He wanted me to thank you again for all the hospitality you've shown him the last week. And for the whole saving my life thing again."

Caleb chuckled.

"I was just paying off a life-saving debt I owed you," he teased. "It's what any good cowboy would do."

Nina laughed as he looped his arm around her shoulders and pulled her closer.

It had been a week since Nina had woken up in the hospital. In that time she'd seen less of Caleb than she had the week they had basically lived together. Between Declan's condition, dealing with the investigation and Nina's father wanting to spend every second with her, they'd only managed to snag a few minutes here and there to talk. Now things were starting to settle again, slowly but surely. Caleb had called her that morning, telling her he'd be at his house around lunch to finally talk about what had happened.

She couldn't deny the idea had been daunting, but now, in the sunshine and the embrace of a charming man, it felt easier.

Caleb must have sensed that, too. He dove in.

"We finally talked to Jay yesterday. The doctor said he'd recover, which seemed to have made him decide he needs to cooperate with us since he's not going anywhere anytime soon and neither are we. Turns out Jeremy approached him in a bar in town where they became fast friends and roommates. Jeremy saw the anger in Jay and exploited it."

"About the house fire when he was younger?"

Caleb nodded.

"That fire was an accident, but when they couldn't afford to rebuild and then had to move, Jay blamed the town for it. The only person he claimed showed them any kindness was Delores when she wrote the article. After that he became obsessed with her. He said he believed that when her stories were above-the-fold it was her way of showing him what was most important to the town. That way he knew what to take from it to make everyone here hurt like he and his mother had. The fire at the restaurant and Gloria's were his way of trying to find a method he enjoyed using to start the fires. But then Delores moved away and he became depressed. He found a friend in Jeremy and even found an apartment near Delores when she came back. Eventually Jay realized that kerosene was his preferred method when he tested it out on the Overlook Pass."

"But what about the fire at your house?" Nina asked. "Fireworks started it."

Caleb ran a hand through his hair.

"This is where it starts to get bananas. Jeremy set the fire at the Gentrys' and the fire at my house while he tasked Jay with following you and taking pictures. Jay said Jeremy told him it would give both of them airtight alibis if the cops ever came looking. Jeremy apparently wasn't that great at using kerosene, though, and burned his arm pretty badly. That's why he switched it up to fireworks on my place. They were easier."

"How does Daniel Covington fit into this, then? What was his role?"

Caleb sighed.

"I think Jeremy was using him as a patsy." He shrugged. "It could have worked, I suppose, had Delores not spooked Daniel into going to confront Jay. He found the kerosene. He already knew about the fireworks and realized that Jeremy was actually targeting you and not just doing some elaborate, petty prank. Daniel went home to pack a bag, worried about retribution, and was ambushed by Jeremy. Jeremy figured out it was Delores who had gotten Daniel to question things and went after her. To Jay that was basically sacrilegious. He was okay with Jeremy dating Delores as a way of keeping her close, but hurting her? Jay wasn't having any of that."

"So that's why he came to get me that day." She realized the truth. Caleb nodded.

"He said he just needed to hide you and use you as leverage so Jeremy would leave Delores alone."

"So who tried to grab me in the barn? Who took all the pictures?"

Caleb's jaw clenched.

"Jeremy took the pictures and Jay was the one who grabbed you. But, according to Jay, it was only meant to scare you. The plan wasn't to actually take you then. Jeremy didn't want to be the one to do it on the off chance you saw him. He would have had a hard time denying it was him behind everything, given your past. The same with the picture taken inside your apartment. Jay freely admitted he picked the lock after Jeremy taught him how."

"Jeremy put so much effort into everything he did," she said. "I wished he would have used that same drive for putting good out into the world instead."

Nina leaned into Caleb's side and shook her head.

"This whole thing *is* bananas."

Caleb chuckled. It rumbled through his body and against hers.

"It is definitely not what *normally* what happens here at the end of Winding Road, never mind Overlook as a whole."

They fell into another small but comfortable silence. The smell of his cologne tickled her senses. It also made her wish they were somewhere more private. She still hadn't properly thanked him for saving her life. Maybe later she could swing it. Despite loving the main house, he'd already complained about living under the same roof as he had growing up while his house was being rebuilt. Now that Nina's father was out of the Retreat, she had a feeling that Caleb might be spending more time there.

Not that she minded at all.

"So, are you going to tell me what's in that big bag you got next to your boots or am I going to have to grab it and run?"

Nina gave a genuine laugh. She'd forgotten she even had it. Leaving his embrace she jumped off the fence and handed it over.

"Desmond and Declan couldn't agree on one color so I decided to veto both of their choices. I thought this just screamed Detective Cowboy."

Caleb pulled out the ivory cowboy hat with a look of surprise that made Nina proud. She'd asked his brothers to keep it a secret when visiting Declan in the hospital. The eldest Nash sibling looked rough but was improving. He had enough sass in him to argue with Desmond as they suggested which hat to get Caleb. In the end she'd had to excuse herself while the two of them launched into one of their silly sibling squabbles, as Madi had affectionately called them.

Caleb ran his hand across the brim of the hat. His smile grew. He put it on.

"I love it," he said simply.

"It definitely works for you."

Caleb laughed and was off the fence in a second flat. He picked Nina up and spun her around. It felt undeniably cheesy and yet unimaginably perfect.

"I can wear it to the Retreat's grand opening party," he exclaimed, all giddy like a child. The party was the next day. After the news had gotten hold of what had forced the Nash family to keep the Wild Iris Retreat closed a little longer, guests had called left and right to rebook. None were angry, which meant Nina still had a job. Not that she wanted it for the same reason she'd had when she accepted it in the first place. "I've even been practicing my dance moves a little bit. I have to admit, you might be more than a little impressed by this fancy-hat-wearing date of yours."

Nina laughed as he twirled her with enthusiasm. Then she was back in his arms. Those true-blue eyes searched her face. He must have liked what he found.

Caleb pulled Nina in for a kiss that she felt throughout her entire body and soul.

Right then and there Nina knew she'd never want

that life under the radar again. Not as long as Caleb was by her side.

He helped her back over the fence and across to his horse. Nina didn't even think to worry when he extended his hand out to her once he was in the saddle.

Instead she took it with a smile, put her foot in the stirrup and let the cowboy and momentum do the rest.

* * * * *

Look for the next book in Tyler Anne Snell's
Winding Road Redemption miniseries,
Credible Alibi, *next month!*

#1863 STEEL RESOLVE
Cardwell Ranch: Montana Legacy • by B.J. Daniels
When Mary Cardwell Savage makes the mistake of contacting her first love, Chase Steele, little does she know that her decision will set off a domino effect that will bring a killer into their lives.

#1864 CALCULATED RISK
The Risk Series: A Bree and Tanner Thriller • by Janie Crouch
Bree Daniels is on the run from a group of genius hackers. Bree seeks refuge in a small town and suddenly finds herself on Deputy Tanner Dempsey's radar. She must protect herself and the two babies her cousin left in her care—but even she knows her heart faces the most risk.

#1865 WYOMING COWBOY BODYGUARD
Carsons & Delaneys: Battle Tested • by Nicole Helm
After country singer Daisy Delaney's stalker kills her bodyguard, Daisy flees to Wyoming. Finding herself under the protection of former FBI agent Zach Simmons, she seems to be safe...but is the person behind the threats someone she trusts?

#1866 KILLER INVESTIGATION
Twilight's Children • by Amanda Stevens
Arden Mayfair hopes to make a fresh start when she returns to her hometown, but soon she finds Reid Sutton—the man she has always loved—on her doorstep, warning her of a recent murder. Signs point to the person who killed Arden's mother, but it couldn't be the Twilight Killer...could it?

#1867 SURVIVAL INSTINCT
Protectors at Heart • by Jenna Kernan
When timid hacker Haley Nobel saves CIA agent Ryan Carr's life, she doesn't know she will become entangled in a perilous mission. Despite Haley's fears, she must work with Ryan to prevent a domestic biohazard attack before it's too late.

#1868 CREDIBLE ALIBI
Winding Road Redemption • by Tyler Anne Snell
Former marine Julian Mercer is shocked when he visits Madeline Nash, the woman he spent an unforgettable week with, only to find her in the back of a squad car. The police think she killed someone, but Julian believes Madi and vows to help her—especially since she's pregnant.

The moment Fiona found the letter in the bottom of Chase's
sock drawer, she knew it was bad news. Fear squeezed the
breath from her as her heart beat so hard against her rib
cage that she thought she would pass out. Grabbing the
bureau for support, she told herself it might not be what she
thought it was.

But the envelope was a pale lavender, and the handwriting
was distinctly female. Worse, Chase had kept the letter a
secret. Why else would it be hidden under his socks? He
hadn't wanted her to see it because it was from that other
woman.

Now she wished she hadn't been snooping around. She'd
let herself into his house with the extra key she'd had made.
She'd felt him pulling away from her the past few weeks.
Having been here so many times before, she was determined
that this one wasn't going to break her heart. Nor was she
going to let another woman take him from her. That's why
she had to find out why he hadn't called, why he wasn't
returning her messages, why he was avoiding her.

They'd had fun the night they were together. She'd felt as if they had something special, although she knew the next morning that he was feeling guilty. He'd said he didn't want to lead her on. He'd told her that there was some woman back home he was still in love with. He'd said their night together was a mistake. But he was wrong, and she was determined to convince him of it.

What made it so hard was that Chase was a genuinely nice guy. You didn't let a man like that get away. The other woman had. Fiona wasn't going to make that mistake, even though he'd been trying to push her away since that night. But he had no idea how determined she could be, determined enough for both of them that this wasn't over by a long shot.

It wasn't the first time she'd let herself into his apartment when he was at work. The other time, he'd caught her and she'd had to make up some story about the building manager letting her in so she could look for her lost earring.

She'd snooped around his house the first night they'd met—the same night she'd found his extra apartment key and had taken it to have her own key made in case she ever needed to come back when Chase wasn't home.

The letter hadn't been in his sock drawer that time.

That meant he'd received it since then. Hadn't she known he was hiding something from her? Why else would he put this letter in a drawer instead of leaving it out along with the bills he'd casually dropped on the table by the front door?

Because the letter was important to him, which meant that she had no choice but to read it.

Don't miss
Steel Resolve *by B.J. Daniels,*
available July 2019 wherever
Harlequin® Intrigue books and ebooks are sold.

Garrett Sterling brought his horse up short as something across the deep ravine caught his eye. A fierce wind swayed the towering pines against the mountainside as he dug out his binoculars. He could smell the rain in the air. Dark clouds had gathered over the top of Whitefish Mountain. If he didn't turn back soon, he would get caught in the summer thunderstorm. Not that he minded it all that much, except the construction crew working at the guest ranch would be anxious for the weekend and their paychecks. Most in these parts didn't buy into auto deposit.

Even as the wind threatened to send his Stetson flying and he felt the first few drops of rain dampen his long-sleeved Western shirt, he couldn't help being curious about what he'd glimpsed. He'd seen something moving through the trees on the other side of the ravine.

He raised the binoculars to his eyes, waiting for them to focus. "What the hell?" When he'd caught movement, he'd been expecting elk or maybe a deer. If he was lucky, a bear. He hadn't seen a grizzly in this area in a long time, but it was always a good idea to know if one was around.

But what had caught his eye was human. He was too startled to breathe for a moment. A large man moved through the pines. He wasn't alone. He had hold of a woman's wrist in what appeared to be a death grip and was dragging her behind him. She seemed to be struggling to stay on her feet. It was what he saw in the man's other hand that had stolen his breath. A gun.

Garrett couldn't believe what he was seeing. Surely, he was wrong. Through the binoculars, he tried to keep track of the two. But he kept losing them as they moved through the thick pines. His pulse pounded as he considered what to do.

His options were limited. He was too far away to intervene and he had a steep ravine between him and the man with the gun. Nor could he call for help—as if help could arrive in time. There was no cell phone coverage this far back in the mountains outside of Whitefish, Montana.

Through the binoculars, he saw the woman burst out of the trees and realized that she'd managed to break away from the man. For a moment, Garrett thought she was going to get away. But the man was larger and faster and was on her quickly, catching her and jerking her around to face him. He hit her with the gun, then put the barrel to her head as he jerked her to him.

"No!" Garrett cried, the sound lost in the wind and crackle of thunder in the distance. After dropping the binoculars onto his saddle, he drew his sidearm from the holster at his hip and fired a shot into the air. It echoed across the wide ravine, startling his horse.

As he struggled to holster the pistol again and grab the binoculars, a shot from across the ravine filled the air, echoing back at him.

Don't miss
Luck of the Draw *by B.J. Daniels, available June 2019*
wherever Harlequin® books and ebooks are sold.

www.Harlequin.com

PHBJDEXP0619